ENTICED

THE ROGUES SERIES BOOK 6

TRACIE DELANEY

Copyright © 2021 Tracie Delaney

Edited by StudioEnp

Proofreading by Katie Schmahl, Jean Bachen, and Jacqueline Beard

Cover art by *Tiffany @TEBlack Designs*

All rights reserved. No part of this publication may be reproduced, stored in any retrieval system, or transmitted, in uniform or by any means, electronic, mechanical, photocopying, recording or otherwise without prior written permission of the author.

This is a work of fiction. Names, characters, places, and incidents are either the products of the author's imagination or are used fictitiously, and any resemblance to actual persons, living or dead, business establishments, events, or locales is entirely coincidental.

BOOK SIX IN THE ROGUES SERIES

Two years ago, the perfect woman walked into my life—on the arm of my brother.

From the moment I saw Trinity Lane, I wanted her, but despite the absolute contempt I have for my brother, there's a code, one I won't break.

Not even the night she lands on my doorstep a quivering wreck and refuses to tell me a damn thing… Or when he comes looking for her with guilt in his eyes.

But sometimes our choices have a habit of exploding in our faces. None more so than the one I made by letting her walk away.

It's the last mistake I'll make. I'll shatter all the rules to keep her safe—and keep us both alive.

A NOTE TO THE READER

Dear Reader,

Oh my. Can you believe it? We're at the last one!

I'm sitting in my office at home writing this with tears in my eyes. I have loved every single minute of this series since the idea of ROGUES first crept into my mind. As each character revealed themselves to me, I fell in love with them and their story. Some surprised me, some irritated me (I'm looking at you, Garen), and some fought me the whole way (hello Upton!) But spending time with these characters has been a privilege, and I'll never forget them.

Sebastian was on the list of characters that surprised me. He's not at all what I thought he would be. Out of the six guys, he was the quietest, but when he began to talk… boy oh boy my heart bled. To meet the woman of your dreams only to find her heart belongs to another—who happens to be your half brother—is a form of torture, and one that Sebastian endures with quiet dignity. Sebastian and Trinity's story is messy and painful, and there is immense suffering on both sides. But their final destination is worth every ounce of pain.

I hope you enjoy spending time with Sebastian and Trinity, as well as catching up with some of the other ROGUES characters. Do message me with your thoughts after you've finished reading, or join my Facebook reader group Tracie's Racy Aces, and take part in the discussion over there.

In the meantime, turn the page and dive in to this final installment. Sebastian and Trinity are waiting for you.

Happy reading.

Love,
Tracie

1

Sebastian

Claws sharper than a grizzly bear's reached into my chest and ripped out my heart as one of my best friends took to the dance floor with his new bride. Not that I didn't share in their joy—I did—but as, one by one, each of the ROGUES had found their happy ever after, it brought into focus the yawning absence of my own.

The problem was, I'd found the right woman. Two years ago, to be exact, at another one of Mother's doomed-to-fail attempts to stitch our broken family back together. The gathering where Trinity Lane walked into my life—on the arm of my half brother. I still recalled with stunning clarity how she'd bowled me over the second I'd laid eyes on her with her classic beauty and throaty laugh. But her intrinsic kindness was the memory that stuck out the most from that night. A member of the catering staff Mom had hired dropped a roasted potato in Trinity's lap, leaving a greasy stain on her dress. Her graciousness and reassurance toward the horrified staff member contrasted starkly with Declan's scowl and sharp words of reprimand. She'd whispered something in his ear, and he'd reddened and offered a stuttering apology to the server. I hadn't looked at another woman since. What was the point in mining for gems when you'd already unearthed a rare, perfect diamond?

Mom and Dad's marriage broke down before I hit my second birthday. She met this English guy at work who'd traveled to New York for a business trip, and that was it. Bye-bye happy family. Hello to always feeling as if both my parents were each tugging on an arm—and pulling in different directions. I'd stayed in America with Dad, while Mom ran off with her shiny new husband. A year after their wedding they welcomed Declan into the world, and I was forgotten amid the endless joy of her perfect life. Worse than that, Declan despised me, and I despised him. It might sound strong to say that, but I refused to hide from the truth. He was lazy, lacked direction, and thought life owed him a living.

I'd never understand how Declan had won Trinity's love. He didn't deserve her. From my viewpoint, he treated her like shit, more so in the past few months. I tried to spend as little time in their company as possible, but sometimes it was unavoidable. On those occasions, I'd track her every movement, my nails drawing blood from my palms as I struggled to keep out of their dysfunctional relationship. Many times I'd come close to squaring up to Declan for the way he spoke to her with such disrespect. They were so fucking mismatched. Declan had a short fuse that had grown considerably shorter in the last few months. Trinity was calm, measured, patient. I applauded her grace in dealing with my sullen half brother, while simultaneously longing to shake some sense into her.

I refrained from declaring my obsession with my brother's girlfriend, although my best friend, Upton, knew. And Oliver, too. Hard to hide much from that wily bastard. But the rest of the ROGUES were oblivious to the planet-sized hole in my chest, too wrapped up in their own lives. Not that I blamed them. I'd sell my soul to the Devil if he promised to stop my heart from going batshit crazy every time I laid eyes on Trinity.

Downing a glass of whiskey that miraculously appeared in front of me, I picked at a scratch in the table and wondered how long I had to stay before it wasn't considered rude to sneak out. I reckoned that I'd wait until Elliot and Sage finished their first dance, and while everyone was busy with their enthusiastic clapping before taking to the dance floor themselves, I'd sneak out while no one was looking. I'd apologize to them later, if necessary.

"They are ridiculously happy."

I glanced up as Upton dragged a chair over for his girlfriend, Belle, and the two of them joined me, uninvited. Not that I minded in the slightest. I didn't get to see much of my best friend. He lived in California, and I lived in London, so popping around for a beer and a chat wasn't exactly in the cards. For a while, we'd lost Upton to a deep depression after a terrorist bomb killed his sister. He'd suffered life-changing injuries himself, and then along came an honest-to-goodness angel who saved him. And for that alone, I'd do anything for Belle. The fact she made him blissfully happy was just another reason to adore the ground she walked on. If anyone deserved joy in their life, it was Upton.

I forced a smile. "They do. I hope Sage knows what she's let herself in for in taking on Elliot." I nudged Belle, drawing a giggle from her. "Tell you what, honey. If this useless bastard doesn't put a ring on it, and soon, what's say you and I waltz down the aisle. Or is it up the aisle? I'm never quite sure."

"Fuck off," Upton retorted with a glower.

I flicked my gaze to Belle and chuckled. "He's so easy to wind up. Offer stands, babe."

Upton growled, and I flashed him an unapologetic grin. "You know what to do."

"And I will. In my own goddamn time."

"Well, do it before I'm old and gray. I've never been a best man, and it's on my bucket list."

"You are such a bullshitter," Upton said.

I signaled to a passing server and requested another round of drinks. Now that Upton and Belle had joined me, it'd make sneaking out harder, so I might as well get pissed instead—on Elliot's dime.

"Are you guys still planning on sticking around in London for a few days?" I asked, hopeful their plans hadn't altered. Usually, whenever there was a get-together, it was me having to travel over to the States. As the only ROGUES board member outside of North America, I guessed it made sense. But when Elliot had surprised Sage with a honeymoon in Europe, they'd decided to have their wedding on this side of the Atlantic, too. As soon as they'd announced they planned to marry in London, I'd used my connections to secure the event space at the top of The Shard. The view from up here was pretty spectacular, even in the depths of winter.

"That's the idea," Upton said. "Unless you've changed your mind about putting us up."

I nodded sagely. "It is a chore. Well, with you, that is. Now, if we're talking about the lovely Belle..." I picked up her hand and kissed the back of it.

"I swear to God, Seb, I'm going to toss you out the window if you don't quit flirting with my girlfriend."

I laughed, a real one. I could always tell the difference. One burst out of me, like a jack-in-the-box, the other felt as if I had to turn my insides out to force a sound that resembled humor.

The dance ended, and Sage gestured for everyone to get up and join them. Friends and family surged onto the dance floor, but Upton and Belle stayed seated.

"Yet another failure," I chided at his reticence to dance. "Are you sure you picked the right friend, Belle?"

"You know as well as I do that I have two left feet," Upton groused.

I laced my fingers, stretched both arms out in front, then cracked my knuckles. "Then you leave me no choice." Standing, I held out my hand to Belle. "Shall we?"

She rose to her feet and pressed her palm to mine. "I'd love to."

I found us a spot on the far side of the dance floor. Slipping my arm around her waist, I took her hand. She tucked her head underneath my chin. "I'm glad we're sticking around for a while."

"Oh, yeah?"

She nodded. "He misses you. And so do I."

"What, this grumpy old face?" I kissed the top of her head. "Give it a few days, and you'll find some excuse to leave early."

"Not a chance."

We fell into a rhythm and simultaneously fell into an accompanying silence. Belle was one of those women who didn't feel the need to chatter on, stuffing every gap in conversation with inane small talk. Yet another plus in her favor, in my view. She used silence well, a tactic that she'd employed on Upton when she'd first started working for him.

I caught Elliot's eye, Sage plastered to his chest as if an invisible magnet connected them. I stuck up my thumb, and he smiled, his face serene and free of the strain he'd carried around for so long while searching for the man who'd kidnapped his sister. Falling in love looked good on him.

My mind drifted back to Trinity. Most days I managed to contain my preoccupation with her, bury it under mounds of paperwork, contract negotiations, and meetings. That way, I kept the wretched loneliness at bay. Today, surrounded by happiness on all sides, that proved impossible to achieve.

The song finished, and I led Belle back to Upton, but as I retook my seat, the urge to leave overcame me again. I'd had enough *happy-happy* for one day. I faked a yawn and downed the last of the whiskey.

"I'm gonna head off, kids," I said. "You've got your key, so just come back whenever you're ready."

"Oh no, stay a bit longer," Belle said.

I leaned down and kissed her cheek. "Laters, sweetheart. I need my beauty sleep."

Upton frowned, two little lines drawing his eyebrows in and down. I knew that look. I took a breath, readying myself for his critique. He stood and fastened his suit jacket.

"I'll walk you out."

And... here it comes.

"Sure."

"Sleep well," Belle said. "See you in the morning."

I pointed my finger at her and made a clicking sound. "You got it."

"You should say goodbye to Elliot at least," Upton said as I headed straight for the elevator.

"Nah, he won't miss me." I pushed the call button. The elevator came immediately, and I strode inside. Upton followed. We reached the lobby without exchanging a word, but as soon as the doors opened and I walked out, Upton grabbed my elbow.

"I don't like leaving you alone. Let me go get Belle and we'll come with you."

"I'm not twelve, Upton." I flicked my wrist dismissively. "Go enjoy the party. No need for my old man ways to spoil the night for you and Belle."

"It's not about that, though, is it?"

I shook my head. "Let's not do this."

"I knew you'd find today difficult." He sighed heavily. "You have to move on eventually."

"Do I? Says who?"

His mouth sloped down at the edges, and a rough sound left his throat. "You're worth more than this. More than spending your life pining after a girl who can never be yours."

I scraped a hand over my chin, stubble scouring my palm despite shaving only this morning. "Don't worry. I have a pretty useful hand as it goes." I flashed him a wide grin, one he didn't return. My smile fell. "Let me do this my way," I said quietly. "Sometimes I go weeks without even thinking of her. It's not like she absorbs my every waking moment. It's just today, that's all. Weddings make me maudlin."

He shoved his fingers through his dark hair, making one side stick up. And then he held out his hand for me to shake. I did.

"Don't get too drunk." I waved and walked away. When I turned around, he'd gone. I stuffed down a bout of loneliness and headed for the taxi stand, jumping into the black cab at the front of the line. I gave my driver my address in Holland Park, rested my head back, and closed my eyes. I must've dropped off to sleep because the next thing I remembered was the cabbie's raised voice rousing me.

"That'll be thirty quid, guvnor."

I fished my wallet from the inside pocket of my tux. I removed two twenty pound notes and handed them over. "Thanks. Keep the change."

He saluted me. "Much appreciated."

I spilled out of the cab and ran my hands over my face. I hated catnapping. It always left me feeling worse than if I'd stayed awake in the first place. I stuffed my hands deep into my pockets, thankful my keys were still in there. Women were so lucky. They had bags for this shit. Not that men couldn't carry a man bag if they wanted to. Course, they'd get ribbed to hell. Despite that, it worked for some.

Why the fuck am I thinking about women's purses? Maybe I'm drunker than I thought.

Chuckling to myself for such bizarre thoughts, I faced the house and walked up the steps at the front. My gaze fell on a figure propped up against the navy-blue front door, their back turned to offer some protection against the elements. I frowned. Holland Park didn't get many homeless people. The police were usually quick to move them on and so they stayed away, frequenting the tourist hotspots where they'd have better luck in pulling in enough cash for a hot meal and maybe a bed for the night. As I reached into my pocket to grab my wallet and give them enough cash to afford decent accommodation for a few nights, they lifted their head.

My mouth dropped open. "Trinity?"

2

Sebastian

Shivering violently, Trinity gazed up at me through her arresting pale-hazel eyes edged with gold flecks. Her cheeks were red from the freezing cold and stained with tears. She jerked upright faster than I could reach out a hand to help her and shoved her hands deep into the pockets of her winter coat.

"I-I..." She stared at her feet, muttered, "Damn it," then continued. "I'm sorry to bother you, Sebastian."

I frowned, then quickly smoothed my expression in case she mistook my concern for irritation at the surprise visit this late at night. "You're not bothering me in the slightest." I dug my keys out of my pocket and opened the door, then motioned for her to go inside. "Let's get you warmed up. It's bitter out here."

I helped her out of her coat and hung it up, then strode through to the kitchen and filled up the electric kettle. In less than two minutes, I'd made her a steaming mug of hot chocolate. She sat at the breakfast bar, wrapped her hands around the mug, and blew across the top of the liquid, then sipped. "Thank you."

"Not a problem."

I leaned casually against the kitchen countertop and waited for her to tell me why she was here. We might not see each other very often—partly because I preferred not to spend more time than necessary in my brother's company, only capitulating when Mom forced my hand with the kind of emotional blackmail she excelled at—but every time I saw Trinity, the gaping hole in my chest widened. I tried not to allow myself to sink into a futile pity party over losing a woman who was never mine to begin with, but on an occasion like today when I'd witnessed Elliot and Sage's blissful union, I found it nigh on impossible not to. After searching my entire life, I'd finally found the one woman I'd give up everything for—and she'd met Declan first.

It would smart like hell even if he was worthy of her, but he wasn't. To an outsider looking in, she might as well be nothing more than Declan's pretty trinket rather than a precious gem that deserved to take center stage. If she were mine, I'd make sure she knew I'd always put her first.

But she isn't—and never will be.

Families lived by a code, one I wouldn't break, no matter the cost to me personally. A brother did not move in on his brother's woman, regardless of their personal antipathy.

She blinked, took in my formal attire, then pushed to her feet. "God, I'm sorry. I shouldn't have come. It's late, and you've obviously been somewhere important. You must be tired."

"It's fine. And it's not that late."

Unless you're a woman walking the streets of London at this hour. Where the fuck was Declan? What the hell was he thinking letting her wander around alone in the middle of the night? Anything could have happened to her.

She released a deep, weighted sigh and, after what

appeared to be an internal war with herself, she retook her seat. Another thirty seconds passed, and still she didn't explain the reason for her visit. I drummed my fingers on the countertop, then shoved them into my trouser pockets. Showing any signs of impatience wouldn't encourage her to talk, but her continued silence caused a spike in my own anxiety.

"Why don't you start with telling me why you're here, and what I can do to help?"

She sipped her hot chocolate, capturing a dribble that ran down the side of the mug with her fingertip. When she sucked on her finger, I almost groaned. If this was anyone else, I'd accuse them of flirting, but Trinity wasn't that kind of girl. This was the first time we'd ever been alone together, and it was killing me. If she kept nibbling on her lip like that, I was liable to kiss her stupid and fuck the consequences.

"I hate to ask, Sebastian, but..." She gave me those absorbing eyes once more. "Can I stay the night? Just tonight. I'll leave first thing in the morning."

I briefly closed my eyes, rubbing two fingers over my mouth. The idea of Trinity under my roof, even for a few hours, was both a dream and a nightmare. I wouldn't get a wink of sleep knowing she was only a few feet away and there was nothing I could do about it.

"Have you and Declan had a row?"

She shook her head.

"Then why do you need a place to stay?"

A swallow forced its way down her throat, but the answer I expected never came. We descended into silence. I folded my arms across my chest and waited.

"Declan has friends over."

She spoke so quietly, for a second, I thought I'd imagined it. A prickle of foreboding crept down my spine, and the back of my neck tingled. It wasn't so much what she said, but how she said it with a tremor to her voice and a bleakness in her eyes. Whoever these friends were, they'd spooked her.

"And that's a problem because?" I coaxed.

She pushed away the half-finished mug of hot chocolate and risked a glance up at me, one she quickly averted.

"I don't like them."

If it were anyone else, I'd laugh and say lots of people don't like my friends either and to just ignore them, but this was Trinity, and I wasn't about to belittle her obvious distress, nor send her back to a place she clearly didn't feel comfortable. Trinity wasn't one of those hard-as-nails women, but she wasn't a scared little mouse either. She wouldn't be very good at her job as an addiction counsellor, where she'd likely come across some challenging and potentially violent characters, if she frightened easily. But normally, there was a quiet steeliness about her, and yet tonight, she couldn't seem to stop her hands from shaking.

"Have you seen these friends before?"

She nodded.

I ground my teeth. If he'd brought shit to her door with another one of his get-rich-quick schemes, I'd kill him.

"Is Declan in some kind of trouble?"

She didn't answer. I tried again, ensuring my tone remained calm and even.

"You can talk to me. I'm here to help."

She lifted her chin, and for a moment, I thought she might tell me what was really going on. And then the shutters came down.

"Not that I'm aware of."

I drilled her with a hard stare. She held it for mere seconds, then looked down. The tip of her finger drew figures of eight on my granite countertop. I breathed out noisily through my nose. Fine. If Trinity wouldn't furnish me with answers, I'd get them from Declan.

"You stay here and finish your drink. I'll go put some fresh towels out in one of the spare rooms for you."

I walked past her, and her hand shot out and touched my wrist. Electricity fired up my arm, straight to my heart. I froze on the spot and risked a glance down at her. God, she was so beautiful with her luminous gold-flecked eyes, her full, ruby-red lips, her button nose with a slight turnup at the end, and her thick glossy hair the color of walnuts that had sun-kissed streaks running through it. Just looking at her broke me. She should have been mine.

"Thank you, Sebastian," she whispered.

A knife twisted in my gut. She wouldn't thank me if she knew the truth.

I nodded. "No problem."

She dropped her hand, and I mourned the loss of her touch even as I briskly strode away to put some distance between us. My only saving grace was the size of this house. I'd put her in the farthest bedroom from my own. That way I could pretend she wasn't here.

Good luck with that.

I laid a stack of towels on top of the bed and left one of my T-shirts there, too. She didn't have a bag with her, and the thought of her sleeping naked in a bed I owned was just too much for me to handle. Even so, I knew that I'd never wash that T-shirt. From tomorrow night, I'd probably sleep with the damn thing underneath my pillow, falling asleep each night with the scent of Trinity all around me. Vanilla and peach. Those were the smells that always came to mind when I passed close enough to Trinity to pick them up. Not that I allowed myself to get that close to her very often. It was safer that way.

Jogging back downstairs, I found Trinity standing by the bi-fold doors looking out onto the backyard bathed in a buttery yellow light. A bird or a fox must have set off the security lights. A few seconds later, darkness descended.

"I can show you up to your room if you like."

She pivoted and gave me a wan smile. "I really do appreciate this, Sebastian. I'm so sorry to put you out like this."

"It's fine," I lied. Having Trinity Lane sleep under my roof was far from fine. God must be having a hell of a joke at my expense.

She trailed after me up the stairs. I turned right and walked to the end of the long hallway. I opened the door to the bedroom and gestured for her to go on in. "There are toiletries in the bathroom, and I left you one of my T-shirts to sleep in."

"Thank you." She sank onto the bed as if she couldn't hold her weight for a second longer. "You're a good man, Sebastian."

Wrong. A good man wouldn't have the kind of thoughts I was having. Thoughts of following her inside, locking the door, stripping her bare, and fucking my brother right out of her head. Fanciful desires. Pipe dreams. A waste of time.

"Sleep well."

I closed the door—with me on the wrong fucking side—and returned downstairs before I made the biggest mistake of my life. As much as it pained me to admit it—and however much I despised him—Declan was family, my mother's son, just as I was my mother's son. There were certain loyalties I refused to break, ones that spoke to the kind of man I aspired to be, the kind of man my father had brought me up to be. And making a move on my brother's girlfriend broke every rule in the book.

Not going to happen. Not today, not tomorrow. Not ever.

The wood burning stove glowed with reds and oranges, pumping welcome heat into my sitting room. I removed my jacket, poured a brandy, and slumped into my favorite chair. Loosening my bow tie, I unfastened the top button on my shirt and locked my gaze on the amber liquid. Trinity Lane was in my house. Right now she was probably undressing and sliding her athletic, long-limbed body between sheets that *I* owned...

Stop! Jesus Christ.

I knocked back the brandy in one swallow, the welcome burn a momentary distraction from the torture of having the object of my obsession so very close, yet farther away than ever. I pulled my thoughts from her and switched them to my brother. I'd planned to go sightseeing with Upton and Belle tomorrow, but that would have to wait. First, a visit to Declan was in order. One way or another, he'd give me the answers I sought.

A commotion in the hallway was followed by Belle's unmistakable giggle. Despite my own troubles, that girl always brought a smile to my lips. I put down the empty glass and went to greet them.

"You're earlier than I expected." I took one look at them both and added, "and drunker."

Belle giggled again. "Blame your friend. It was his idea to line up the tequila shots."

She wobbled, saved only by Upton's quick reactions.

"Time for bed, beautiful."

"Now you're talking," she leered.

I covered my ears. "Please."

She grinned, then patted Upton's chest. "Will you get me a glass of water? I'll warm the bed, lover."

"Seriously, Belle," I admonished.

Upton guided her to the stairs, making sure she had a firm grip on the handrail. "Go on up. I'll be a couple of minutes."

Watching her make her way upstairs was like witnessing a newborn foal find its legs.

"You're a terrible drunk," I called after her.

She showed me her middle finger.

I chuckled, then followed Upton into the kitchen. As soon as we were alone, I dropped the bombshell.

"Trinity's here."

Upton's chin almost hit the floor. "Why? When?"

"She was waiting for me when I got home. Asked to stay the night."

"She had a fight with Declan?"

"I'm not sure. She says not, but something's going on. Whatever it is, she refuses to tell me much other than he had a few friends over and she didn't like them."

"Sounds fishy."

I nodded. "I know I said I'd go sightseeing with you both tomorrow, but can you amuse yourselves for the day? I need to talk to Declan and find out what the fuck is going on."

Upton clapped a hand on my shoulder. "You do what you need to do. I can read a map."

"You sure about that?" I teased. "Thanks. I appreciate it. See you in the morning."

I pivoted and walked away.

"Hey, Seb?"

Glancing back, I locked eyes with my best friend, his face painted with sorrow.

"Yeah?" I husked.

"I'm sorry, man."

I shrugged. "So am I."

3

TRINITY

I opened my eyes to lilac walls and the weight of an impossibly soft cotton quilt covering me. I blinked, waiting for my vision to clear and the fog of a deep sleep to lift.
Where am I?
I blinked again, then rubbed my eyes.
Oh God...
Last night's events came back in a rush. I forced a breath through a tight chest and sat up. Groaning, I shoved my fingers through my tangled hair. Of all the places I could have run off to, Sebastian's home should not have made the list. Dammit. Why didn't I check in to a hotel, even if I couldn't afford it? Or hunkered down at an all-night cinema and waited for dawn to arrive? Anywhere would have been better than to land myself on Sebastian's doorstep. The resolute grit in his eyes when we'd spoken last night along with my taciturn responses had left him with more questions than answers, questions he'd put to

Declan. Questions Declan would refuse to answer—meaning all hell would break loose.

Trinity, what the heck have you done?

My relationship with Declan was already teetering on the edge of disaster, and my coming here had put another nail in the coffin. When we first met, I thought he was the one, but during the last year or so, he'd changed, and now, I hardly recognized the man who'd swept me off my feet with flowers and champagne and promises of a bright future together.

All I'd ever wanted was a family. Growing up in an orphanage after both my parents died a week before my tenth birthday had left me with a burning need to replace what I'd lost. Adoption wasn't in the cards for a child like me. No one wanted the older kids. They all wanted cute babies or toddlers. Once you hit four or five, you'd better get used to life in the system, because no one was coming to save you.

But Declan had made me feel special, and his mum and dad had welcomed me with open arms. Finally, I felt like I belonged somewhere—until it all started to change. I couldn't even say with certainty when I'd noticed that Declan was growing more withdrawn, more secretive. It kind of crept up on me until his behavior—odd at first, then turning bitter and nasty—became the norm, and the man I once thought I knew dissolved into a memory that felt more like a dream than reality.

Throwing back the covers, I padded over to the bathroom and stared at myself in the mirror. I looked tired, the insomnia that had plagued me for months scoring dark circles beneath my eyes. Funnily enough, last night was the first time in ages where I slept right through. But with the inevitable dawn came the reckoning—and one I had to face head-on. Maybe I could go for damage control, give Sebastian a little of the truth mingled with enough lies to stop him digging too deeply. At this point, anything was worth a try.

I wondered whether Declan had even noticed me sneak out the front door last night. When this particular bunch of guys came to visit, they'd spend the night playing cards, drinking, and snorting coke, and I'd usually make myself scarce, hiding in the bedroom until they left. But last night, something had been off. An undercurrent of bad vibes that had urged me to flee. And so I had. Sebastian had been a terrible choice, but with limited funds at my disposal, I didn't exactly have a lot of options for somewhere to spend the night.

I hardly knew Sebastian. He and Declan weren't exactly the best of friends, but he had a quiet strength and a warmth about him that called to me on a level I couldn't say I truly understood. He exuded the sort of authority that made me feel safe, but coming here had set in motion a steamroller I had no idea how to stop from running over us all.

With a resigned sigh, I quickly showered, dressed, and headed downstairs. I wished I could leave before Sebastian realized I was even out of bed, but if I were to stand a chance of stopping him from grilling Declan, then I had to face the music. Instead of lying, I'd decided begging made for a better choice.

Voices greeted me, filtering from the direction of the kitchen. Sebastian must have company. I thought I'd heard people talking last night right before I'd drifted off to sleep, but when the house had fallen silent, I'd assumed I'd imagined them. God, now I felt even worse about bursting in on him last night. I had no right to interrupt his life and dump my problems on his doorstep.

I tentatively crept along the hallway and peered around into the kitchen.

Oh crap.

What's Declan's mum doing here?

I took two steps back. Too late. Sebastian saw me and beckoned.

"Morning, Trinity."

At Sebastian's greeting, Serena glanced over her shoulder, and she didn't appear in the least bit surprised to find me in the wrong son's house. She smiled warmly and patted the seat beside her.

"Morning, darling. Sebastian said you were here. Would you like tea or coffee?"

"Um, tea would be lovely, thank you."

I shot Sebastian a questioning look, wanting him to give me some idea of what he'd told his mother, but he either ignored me on purpose, or he misread my wide-eyed plea.

"Sebastian tells me you and Declan have had a misunderstanding," Serena said. "You could have come to me, you know. You're always welcome at my house."

I tilted my head to the side. She had a point. I was far closer to Serena and Justin, Declan's father, than I was to Sebastian. So why had I darkened his door with my troubles? I could have made anything up if I'd gone to Serena's house and she'd have believed me. But Sebastian was a whole other prospect.

How could I tell a doting mother my worries that her beloved son, egged on by his friends, had progressed from flirting with coke to become a full-on addict? Or worse, that I had a suspicion he was dealing, too?

"Just a little one. It's nothing."

I wrapped my arms around my middle and glanced at Sebastian out of the corner of my eye. His steely gray gaze filled with compassion and... something else I couldn't put my finger on. But whatever that something was, it caused an alien sensation to ripple up my spine, a not unpleasant feeling. With some difficulty, I refocused my attention on Serena.

"I'd be grateful if you didn't say anything to him. You know how proud he is, and he won't appreciate me blabbing about our private life." Not that what I'd told either of them could count as blabbing.

"Proud?" Sebastian clenched his jaw, the earlier compassion I'd witnessed draining from his eyes. "Stubborn more like. And while I have no desire to get in the middle of whatever is going on between you and my brother, you came to me, Trinity, and there's a reason for that. Has he or any of his so-called friends hurt you?"

"No," I cried. "God, no. Not at all. Declan wouldn't do that."

"And his *friends*?"

"No." I spoke softly, my eyes lowering to the floor. "They just spooked me, that's all. I overreacted." I didn't overreact, but I'd say just about anything to avoid Sebastian digging deeper. The truth was that those men had scared me. Their joviality had felt false, as if at any minute, the tide could turn. That suggestion alone had driven me out of my home and into Sebastian's.

"Well, if you're not willing to tell me, then I guess I'll have to ask Declan."

A chill seated itself in my bones. As an addiction counsellor, I understood better than most that backing an addict into a corner was the worst thing you could do. If Declan was in as deep as I feared, then I was best placed to coax him into accepting help, and if I succeeded, then his family would be none the wiser.

"Please don't," I pleaded. "Let me handle Declan."

Sebastian set a jug of milk on the breakfast bar. "Too late."

Serena shot me an apologetic half smile as she poured my tea. "I texted him, darling. I didn't want him worrying about where you were. He's on his way over."

Oh, hell. My stomach flipped. I never should have come here. I'd made things ten times worse, and Declan would blame me for involving his family in our personal affairs. Or rather *his* personal affairs, ones that, if my worries were true, were the last thing he'd ever want his brother or his parents to know about.

Of course, I could be wrong. He was using drugs—extensively—but I had no actual proof of him dealing, just a lot of dubious activity and comings and goings by all kinds of strange individuals including those guys from last night, who Declan had described as his "business partners".

Unlike Sebastian, Declan wasn't a wealthy man. Far from it. He wheeled and dealed, and dabbled in lots of different things. We only got by because of my steady income as a counsellor. Declan was always chasing the next big thing, determined that one day he'd trump his brother's success. At the beginning of our relationship, he'd been full of ideas, and I'd found his boundless energy and enthusiasm attractive. That Declan had been so exciting to spend time with. But as the months passed, I learned that none of his grandiose plans ever came to fruition, a problem he laid at Sebastian's door, although I'd never understood how it was his brother's fault that Declan hadn't found the success he craved.

A few minutes later, a knock came at the door, and I didn't need to see through to the other side to know who it was.

"I'll get it," I said.

"Stay where you are."

Sebastian's tone, laced with a command I didn't dare ignore, froze me in place. The billionaire CEO was in full flow as he strode past me and down the hallway. I wrapped my hands around my mug of tea, more for something to do with them than a desire to drink it.

Serena patted my forearm. "Don't look so worried."

"I don't want to cause any trouble between them."

"You haven't."

I gave her a wan smile, but it didn't last. Footsteps sounded behind me, and low voices grew louder as the two men approached. I sat woodenly, searching Declan's face to try to get a read on his emotions. He'd schooled his expression into a blank canvas, but there was a coldness in his eyes that tied my stomach in knots.

"There you are." Declan reached me in two strides and

kissed my temple, the affectionate gesture in direct contrast to his body language. "You had me worried for a while until Mum texted to let me know you were here." His nostrils flared while his lips flattened in true pissed-off Declan style. "You really shouldn't have bothered Seb."

"I—"

"She wasn't any trouble," Sebastian interjected. "You, on the other hand..."

Declan shifted his angry gaze from me and fired a blazing glare at his brother. "Oh, here we go again." He set his hands on his hips. "Go on, Seb. Do your worst."

Sebastian pressed the tips of his fingers to the breakfast bar, his usually calm, gray eyes swirling with annoyance, reminding me of an approaching storm.

"Why did Trinity feel the need to come here last night, Declan? And don't try to bullshit me with platitudes about having a lover's tiff."

I'd already told Sebastian it was because of Declan's friends, yet he chose not to reveal what he knew to Declan. Evidently, he'd decided to test his younger brother's honesty. My hands curled into fists, my nails digging into my palms until I was sure I'd drawn blood, and no amount of steady breathing calmed my racing heart.

"It's none of your business," Declan hit back.

"You've made it my business."

"Me?" Declan snorted. "I've done jack shit."

"This is my fault." I slid off the chair and laid a hand on Declan's arm, hoping to stave off an impending argument between the brothers. "I shouldn't have come here."

"No, you fucking shouldn't have," Declan spat at me.

Sebastian moved so fast, he blurred right in front of my eyes. Declan retreated, his back hitting the wall. Sebastian crowded in, his face, blooming with color, inches from Declan's. "Don't you dare speak to her like that."

Declan worked his jaw. "Back the fuck up."

I shot a despairing look at Serena, silently begging her to intervene. Whether she'd seen it all before and had almost become immune to their antipathy toward one another, or she simply didn't fancy getting in the middle of two testosterone-fueled men, she remained in her seat, worrying her lip, her eyes fixed on her two sons almost coming to blows.

"You're a mess, Declan. You're rudderless and lazy and you think the world owes you a living."

"Well, I guess we can't all be as perfect as you, hey, Seb? A regular fucking saint, that's what you are."

Sebastian stood taller, giving him a couple of inches on Declan. "Something is going on, and whatever it is, I'll find out, so you might as well tell me. Why did Trinity feel the need to camp outside my house last night in the freezing cold waiting for me to get home rather than spend another second in that flat with you?"

"And I'm only going to say this once more before I break your jaw. *It's none of your business.*"

"Okay, boys, that's enough," Serena finally interjected.

Sebastian stepped back, and I expelled a relieved sigh. I'd started this by coming here, and Declan wouldn't let me forget my mistake in a hurry.

Dumbest decision ever.

"Trinity, get your things," he barked. "We're going home."

Sebastian directed his attention to me. "You don't have to go with him if you don't want to. You can stay here as long as you like."

Declan growled, the sound a warning shot that saw me force a smile and accompany it with a shake of my head. Better that I went with him, waited for him to calm down, and then try to get through to him—again—rather than remain here and pour fuel onto the fire.

"Thank you for putting me up last night. I appreciate it."

Sebastian schooled his expression, the shutters coming down, making it impossible to guess what he was thinking.

"You're welcome here anytime," he said softly.

Declan gripped my elbow. "Mum, I'll call you." He shot a final irate glare at Sebastian. "And you. Stay the fuck away from my girl."

4

Trinity

Declan didn't utter a single word on the journey home, but the tic in his jaw and the way his hands gripped the steering wheel were all the signs I needed to know that I wasn't in his good books. Fine. He wasn't in mine either. I twisted in my seat, giving him my back, and stared out the window. If he expected me to apologize, then he was in for a very long wait. I had nothing to apologize for. If he hadn't invited those... degenerates over to our flat, then I wouldn't have felt unsafe. Choosing to bed down for the night at Sebastian's might not have been my finest decision, but it was his friends who had driven me to leave in the first place.

It took a little over half an hour to drive home, and by the time Declan pulled on the handbrake and cut the engine, the atmosphere was as thick and heavy as a slice of his mother's chocolate fudge cake. I jumped out of the car and stomped to the front door, remembering too late that I'd forgotten my key when I'd walked out last night. I folded my arms and waited for Declan to open up.

The flat stank of sweat and cigarette smoke, and when I caught sight of the living room, I almost wept. Pizza boxes strewn everywhere, half-drunk cans of beer spilling their remains all over my couch, at least two cigarette burns in the carpet—which meant we'd lose our deposit on the flat.

I went straight to the kitchen and opened the drawer where we kept the heavy-duty black bin sacks and tore one off at the serrated edge. Shaking it open, I returned to the living room to find Declan sprawled on the chair, his long legs stretched out in front of him.

"You should be cleaning this up, not me," I snapped, crouching to pick up a can that had rolled underneath the couch.

"Whatever," he muttered. "Why did you run off like that, anyway?"

"I've told you before, Declan, I don't like the company you're keeping."

"They're my friends," he offered, his words accompanied by a sullen pout.

"They're drug addicts, Declan, and the way you're headed, you'll end up in the same place as them."

In my professional opinion, he already was a drug addict, but this was yet another gentle attempt to coax him into admitting he had a problem that went much further than a Friday night pick-me-up.

"Clutch your fucking pearls, why don't you, Trinity? Jesus Christ, when did you become such a goody-two-shoes? It's a little coke on the weekends and an occasional splurge in the week after a hard day. What's wrong with that?"

I refrained from telling him there was *everything* wrong with that, not least because we were hardly rolling in cash. Oh, and not forgetting that drugs were illegal. We'd had this argument so many times, I could reel it off verbatim, but it didn't move the dial on Declan's deteriorating behavior. When had it all begun? I couldn't remember. All I knew was that the Declan Hunt belligerently staring at me while I cleaned up the shit from the impromptu party he and his druggie mates had last night, and the Declan I first met two years ago were unrecognizable from each other.

Not for the first time, I mulled over my choices. If I told Declan's parents, or even—God forbid—Sebastian, that Declan was keeping bad company, they'd step in and maybe save him from the path he seemed determined to tread. Yet I knew with one hundred percent certainty that if I did that, Declan would never speak to me again and I'd lose the family I'd craved since I was a little girl. Sometimes a poisonous relationship was better than no relationship at all.

Christ, am I really that desperate to belong?

I cleared away the mess and put the living room back into some semblance of order, and by the time I returned from putting the rubbish outside ready for collection the next day, Declan had fallen asleep with his mouth partly open, his loud snores grating on my few remaining nerves. Snoring. Another habit I'd noticed he'd developed since his drug taking had ramped up a notch.

My hands clenched into fists. I tamped down my urge to knock his elbow off the chair as I marched past. Another bad-tempered fight wouldn't help. I needed to calm down and have an adult conversation with him once he woke up. A walk would help. I reached for a throw off the back of the couch and laid it over him, scribbled a note to tell him where I'd gone, and quietly closed the door.

An hour later, cold and damp from the constant drizzle, I arrived home. Declan greeted me with an apologetic smile.

"I'm sorry I yelled at you."

Sighing heavily, I perched on the arm of the chair and

brushed a lock of hair out of his eyes. His skin felt clammy, and as I peered closer, the worry lines that had arrived a couple of months ago seemed to have scored even deeper into his skin. He looked like a man with the weight of the world on his shoulders.

"I'm concerned about you, Declan. You've changed. Please let me put you in touch with someone who can help with your addiction."

His brief conciliatory tone vanished, and his eyes hardened. "You're the one who's changed, Trinity. The constant nagging and pecking at my head is driving me insane. I'm not a fucking addict, all right?"

"See what I mean?" I splayed my arms out wide. "The Declan I used to know wouldn't have reacted like that."

"Oh, fuck off, Trinity." He launched to his feet, grabbed his coat and his keys, and stomped to the door.

"Where are you going?"

"Somewhere I can get some fucking peace."

The front door slammed, and the room descended into silence. Exhausted, I collapsed onto the couch. Arguing with Declan always sapped my energy, and this latest spat was no different. I kept hoping he'd change, revert to the man I'd first met and fallen for… funny, affectionate, enthusiastic about life and the future. Yet every day, he grew more and more distant. The Declan I once knew no longer existed. I'd tried to help him, to get through to him and use my professional skills to shine a light on the truth, but everything I did seemed to make things worse. Had my childhood experiences damaged me to the extent that I clung to a relationship with a man I didn't even like anymore, yet alone love?

My stomach growled. With nothing of substance to eat, I picked up my purse and headed out to the local supermarket. I picked up enough food to last three or four days and stood in line at the checkout. The queue moved at a snail's pace. Eventually I reached the front and loaded my items onto the belt. The teenager serving me didn't even make eye contact. Too busy scanning the barcodes and chewing gum, her jaw moving at a record pace.

"Twenty-seven thirty," she said as I packed the last of the items.

I opened my purse, and my stomach dropped. The fifty pounds I'd withdrawn from the ATM last week was gone—and only one person could have taken it.

Declan.

With a sigh, I inserted my card into the chip and pin machine. My salary wasn't due for another week, which meant although I had enough in the bank to pay for this shop, I'd have to dip into my overdraft to see me through to payday, something I hated doing. Growing up with nothing, I was very frugal with my money. The idea of going back to living hand to mouth and struggling to afford the smallest luxuries wasn't a pleasant thought.

"Sorry, it's been declined."

I blinked, certain I'd misheard. "Excuse me?"

The checkout operator blinked at me as if I was stupid. She blew a bubble, the gum snapping back against her lips. "Your bank has refused the card."

"I-I don't understand."

"Hey, lady," the guy behind me said. "Can you hurry up? Some of us have places to be."

My face bloomed with embarrassment. Fishing out my emergency credit card, I inserted it into the machine. Thankfully, that payment went through, and I hustled out of the shop as fast as possible.

Crossing the street, I stood in line at the ATM. I had a one thousand pound approved overdraft that I'd arranged a few months ago in case of a genuine emergency. There shouldn't have been any issue with payment. Finally my turn arrived, and

I put my card into the machine and asked for a balance. The machine whirred and spat out a slip of paper. I scanned it.

No. That's not possible.

The balance read minus four thousand, nine hundred and ninety-eight pounds.

I swayed, and my hand shot out, bracing against the wall to support my weight. I didn't understand. Banks weren't risk-takers. The most they'd let you go overdrawn was up to the limit of your arranged overdraft. So why was mine over by almost four times my agreed limit of one thousand pounds? On wobbly legs, I staggered into the branch right across the street and lined up to speak to a member of the staff.

Ten minutes later, I lurched back outside, chilled to the bone, and not only because of the freezing temperatures. Declan had—without my knowledge or permission—applied for an increase to my overdraft limit. The bank had approved it because I had a decent credit rating, and then Declan must have withdrawn the entire sum. I'd had to play dumb with the bank clerk, given that what Declan had done amounted to fraud. I wasn't even sure how he'd accomplished it. The clerk must have thought I'd lost my mind when I had to pretend I'd not only forgotten I'd organized the increased overdraft, but that I'd forgotten I'd withdrawn the money as well.

Numb with shock, I traipsed home, practicing what I'd say to Declan. The stolen money lent further credence to my theory that he wasn't only using drugs, but dealing them as well.

What have you done?

Declan wasn't home when I arrived. I sat in the chair that faced the door and waited. Night had fallen by the time I heard a scuffle outside the door and Declan stumbled inside reeking of alcohol and cigarette smoke.

"Where have you been?" I gritted out between teeth that locked together. My jaw ached from clamping them shut.

He scrubbed a hand over his face. "Don't start, Trinity," he slurred. "I've had a shitty day."

"I'll hazard a guess it wasn't as shitty as mine."

He narrowed his eyes in that way drunks did when they were trying to focus. "Who's bitten your arse?"

"I went to the bank today."

I counted three seconds before he realized I knew. He slumped to the sofa and buried his head in his hands.

"I'm sorry," he mumbled.

"Declan, it's *five thousand pounds*. How on earth am I going to pay that back?"

"I'll take care of it."

"How?" I stood and walked over to him, then squatted. "Are you going to ask Sebastian to bail you out? Because unless that's your plan, I have no idea how we're going to afford to pay back such a sum anytime soon."

Declan glared up at me with red-rimmed eyes and an even redder face. "I don't want shit from that bastard," he snapped. "I told you I'll take care of it, and I will. I've had a run of bad luck, that's all."

A run of bad luck? Is he gambling, too?

He scrambled upright and stomped off to bed. I rose to my feet and stared after him with a mixture of fury and fear. Maybe the time had come to involve his parents before he destroyed not just himself, but me as well.

But even as those thoughts seeped into my mind, I knew I couldn't do it. I'd loved Declan once, and while he'd gradually killed that love over the last few dreadful months, I couldn't bring myself to leave him, not when he needed me the most. To abandon an addict at a time of great need went against every instinct I had, both professional and personal. One way or another, I must find a way to reach him.

The problem was, I didn't know how.

5

SEBASTIAN

"I can't believe how fast the last two weeks have gone," Belle said as I lifted their bags from the trunk of the car outside the departure terminal at Heathrow Airport. She wrapped me in a tight hug. "Thank you for putting up with us. Come and visit us soon, won't you?"

I kissed the top of her head. "Try and stop me. And remember," I said, casting a sidelong glance at Upton accompanied by an impish grin, "if this dickhead doesn't propose soon, it's you and me walking down the aisle."

Belle giggled while Upton glowered, causing me to belt out a laugh. His senseless jealousy always brought a smile to my face. I happened to know he had a proposal all worked out, one he planned to execute tomorrow at the top of the Eiffel Tower in Paris. Belle didn't have a clue, but there wasn't a doubt in my mind she'd accept. My best friend had discovered an absolute diamond of a woman, but at the same time, she'd gotten a great deal, too. Upton Barrick was a good man, one of the best.

"You gonna be okay?" Upton asked.

I flashed a brilliant smile. "Why wouldn't I be?"

Upton gave me his silent version of "What utter bullshit" accompanied by an arched eyebrow and a disparaging quirk to his lips.

"I'll be in touch."

He clapped me on the back, took Belle's hand, and the two of them soon became enveloped by the throngs of people heading inside the terminal building. I stood there for a moment or two, reflecting on how they'd taken my mind off my troubles, but now that they'd gone, loneliness and a sense of despair overwhelmed me. I hadn't heard a thing from either Trinity or Declan since they'd left my house eleven days ago. Not that I expected to. I saw my half brother a total of six times last year, and Trinity only four. It wasn't unusual to go for months without our paths crossing at all. But this time was different. I smelled trouble, and now that my guests had left, I had the time to devote to finding out what my brother was up to, who these friends of his were, and why they'd agitated Trinity so much, she felt it necessary to come to me for shelter, knowing the trouble her decision would cause with Declan.

Declan infuriated me. He was a bright guy, but he wasted his intelligence on get-rich-quick schemes that never quite came off. If he put his energies into more valuable pursuits, he'd achieve the wealth he'd craved ever since I and the rest of the ROGUES board hit the big time over thirteen years ago now. On several occasions, I'd offered to bankroll a start-up company once he came up with a legitimate and well-thought-through business plan.

He never had.

The problem with my brother, as I'd inadvisably pointed out to him the other week, much to Mother's chagrin as she eloquently told me afterward, was that he lacked the drive needed to succeed in the commercial world. He wanted it all to land in his lap without working for it. Sure, I'd had a stroke of luck, but if we'd ridden off the back of that one success story, our business would have died long ago. Instead, we'd diversified, looked for new opportunities, and worked our backsides off to turn ROGUES from a one-trick pony into a global phenomenon. But Declan never saw the work required, only the end result, and therefore, he assumed he could shortcut it and still be successful.

I caught sight of the parking attendant frowning in my direction and hopped into my car before he gave me a ticket. I made my way out of the airport and joined the M4 motorway. Met with a sea of red brake lights, I pulled off at the first available opportunity and took an alternative route home, one that wouldn't see me sitting in traffic for hours on end.

The house was eerily quiet without Upton and Belle there to fill the silence that had been my constant before they'd arrived a few days ahead of Elliot and Sage's wedding. I didn't mind my own company, yet I felt their absence keenly. I had a contract review that needed my attention but, unusually, the idea of work didn't appeal. Instead, I decided to go for a walk to try to clear my head. London was having one of those rare January days where the air was cold and crisp, the sky a brilliant blue, and a light frost covered the usually damp pavements, giving a crunch underfoot.

I made my way through Holland Park and crossed Kensington High Street, then continued down Cromwell Road. My mind whirred with all manner of things, haphazardly jumping from one thought to the next. Without being aware of where I was headed, I found myself on King's Road, and only then did I realize exactly what I'd done.

Trinity's offices were on King's Road.

I stared across the street at the red-brick building with its Georgian windows and colorful window boxes filled with winter pansies. I lost count of how long I stood there watching people come and go. I ached, deep inside my chest. No amount of money would bring me the one thing I wanted above all else.

"Sebastian?"

I whirled around and inwardly groaned. The object of my yearning stood before me, a soft frown drawing her eyebrows low.

"What are you doing here?"

My mind raced trying to conjure up a reasonable excuse for loitering outside her place of work, but every one sounded ridiculous and as see-through as a freshly cleaned pane of glass. My subconscious had brought me here, but I'd intentionally stayed when I should have fled, all in the hope I'd catch a glimpse of her and provide some much needed sustenance to feed my craving.

"I wanted to see how things were. I've been worried about you."

She glanced at her feet, then tilted back her head, gazing up at me with despairing eyes.

"I'm okay."

Her words, accompanied with how haunted she appeared, fired up my instincts. She wasn't okay. Far from it.

"Are you?"

She averted her gaze and returned her attention to the cold, gray sidewalk.

"Trinity?"

"Things have been difficult, but we'll get through it. We always do."

I wish you wouldn't.

I shuffled my feet, immediately cursing myself for having such thoughts, no matter their brevity. "Let me help. Whatever it is, we can fix it. Nothing's insurmountable."

She shook her head violently. "You know how Declan is, Sebastian."

All too well.

"How about a coffee?"

Sighing, she checked her watch. "I can't. I have an appointment. I'm on my way there now."

"I'll walk with you," I said, unwilling to let her go so soon.

She nodded and set off with me falling into step beside her. We meandered along in silence, but I didn't care. I craved her company, to be close enough that we were almost touching. Conversation was a side bonus, and if she preferred quiet, that was fine by me.

A few minutes later, she veered off the King's Road and into a quiet, leafy street lined with Georgian houses on one side and Victorian houses on the other. She stopped outside a three-story building with a bright-red front door and a small front yard paved in Cotswold stone.

"This is me."

I tilted my head to the side and raised my eyebrows. "I wouldn't have thought there was much call for your particular skill set in a well-to-do neighborhood like this."

She guarded her eyes from the weak winter sunshine and looked up at me. "You'd be surprised. None of us knows what goes on behind closed doors."

How true. "Indeed."

She offered me a faint smile that didn't last. "Thank you for coming to check on me."

"You're welcome."

She put her hand on the iron gate, then paused. Turning back to me, she opened her mouth, closed it, and then sighed.

"If you have time this weekend to call by the flat and have a talk with Declan, I'd appreciate it."

At last! She'd finally asked for help. I nodded enthusiastically. "Absolutely. How about tomorrow, first thing? Say nine?"

"Sounds good."

She went through the gate and knocked on the door. Moments later, a woman in her early thirties answered and motioned for Trinity to come inside. I waited until she disappeared, then took a circuitous route home, mulling over what she'd said about closed doors and guessing that she'd been talking about herself more than her client, or maybe as well as her client.

Whatever troubles she had with my brother, I would get to the bottom of them. And with Trinity reaching out, I finally had the excuse I'd been waiting for.

6

Trinity

I wrestled my way onto the packed Tube and only narrowly avoided losing my head as the train doors slammed closed. Barely able to breathe, it occurred to me that animal transports had more safeguards in place than humans did on the godforsaken London Underground at rush hour. The smell of body odor hung in the air, and as the crowds closed in, I shuffled forward, bumping into an elderly lady clinging to the leather straps hanging down from the train ceiling.

"Sorry," I said.

"Don't worry, dear." She smiled kindly. "Long day?"

Normally I avoided engaging in conversation with randoms on the Tube. London, like most major cities, was full of oddities, and chatting could encourage unwanted dialogue. But this little old lady was probably a safe bet.

"Very."

"I bet you're looking forward to getting home and putting your feet up."

"I am," I lied.

In truth, I dreaded walking through the door. After finding out that Declan had defrauded me of five thousand pounds, I dug further into our finances and discovered that he'd maxed out his credit cards and stripped his own bank account, too. All totaled, we owed thirteen and a half thousand pounds. To whom? I didn't have a clue. Declan refused to tell me, but in the last week and a half, he'd grown even more withdrawn, snapping at me every time I opened my mouth, and disappearing off only to return at all hours of the night in a worse mood than when he left. He seemed to wear this constant sheen of sweat across his brow, his hair was permanently greasy—which for a man who always prided himself on his appearance was worrying in itself—and he'd aged ten years in the last month. More than once, I'd begged him to go to Sebastian and ask for his help, but he greeted my suggestions with so much yelling, I stopped raising the idea.

Sebastian. God, it had been good to see him today, albeit fleetingly. He had this air about him that exuded calm and made me feel so safe. Cocooned, almost. It had been on the tip of my tongue to tell him my suspicions regarding Declan, but fear for what he might do if I did had made me swallow the words. I could only hope that by asking him to come around and talk to Declan, I hadn't made things a whole lot worse.

Declan had never been violent toward me, but I had to admit that in the last few days, it had crossed my mind that he might be capable of lashing out. On more than one occasion, he'd curled his hands into fists, a vein throbbing in his forehead, and he'd loomed over me with hatred painted on his face whenever I brought up the subject of money—or his brother.

The station before mine usually emptied the train, and tonight was no different. As the majority of passengers disembarked onto the platform, I sank into a seat, even though my stop was only another five minutes away. My feet were killing me, and any chance to rest them was a blessed relief.

I arrived at my stop and headed for the escalator. A barrier lay across the foot of it, and a big yellow sign denoted 'out of order.' Groaning, I hauled myself up three enormous flights of stairs and emerged into a dark and wet night. I put up my hood and bent my head to avoid getting hit in the face with needles of rain.

I reached the flat to find it in darkness, and the bloom of relief that filled my chest told me everything I needed to know about the state of my relationship with Declan. Maybe I would get a chance to put my feet up and enjoy a little quiet reflection before he came home from wherever he'd been and spoiled my peace—or spoiled for an argument. Even when we weren't rowing, the atmosphere, so dense and oppressive, sapped what little energy I had left after a hard day at work dealing with other people's problems when I had a huge number of my own waiting for me at home.

I unlocked the door and felt around for the light switch on the inside wall. Dropping my bag right by the entrance, I kicked off my shoes and collapsed onto the couch.

"Declan," I called out, even though I was pretty certain he wasn't here. When he didn't reply, I released a deep sigh and closed my eyes. I'd almost dropped off when a loud bang jerked me awake. I shot upright, my heart thundering, then laughed at myself when the sound came again and I realized it was only a car backfiring. Someone's vehicle must need a service. Awake now, I decided to run a bath to try to get the kinks out of my tight shoulders. I trudged into the bedroom and turned on the lights.

"Declan! Oh God, no!"

I lurched forward, wrapping my arms around his legs. "Declan. Oh, Declan, please hang on."

I tried to lift him, but he was too heavy. I screamed, fear

sitting across my chest, a dead weight that I couldn't shift. "God, help me! Somebody."

The bed was pushed haphazardly to the side. I hauled it closer, then scrambled onto it. I dug my nails into the knot, where Declan had fastened the rope to the ceiling fan, and tried to loosen it.

"Come on, come on. God, please."

The knot refused to come loose. Sprinting into the kitchen, I snatched a knife from the wooden block. It took ages, too long, but somehow I sawed through the thick rope.

"Don't you dare die on me, Declan Hunt. You hear me!"

Tears streamed down my face as Declan slumped to the mattress. I fell to my knees beside him and yanked the rope from around his neck. His face was swollen, his tongue hung out of his mouth, and an awful purple and red mark encircled his throat where the twine had dug into his skin.

"Oh God, Declan," I sobbed. "What have you done?"

I checked for a pulse, already knowing I wouldn't find one. I had no idea how long he'd been here, but it was too late to save him. His vacant eyes stared up at me, bulging out of his head. I tried to close them, but they wouldn't stay shut.

"I'm sorry. I'm so sorry."

I pressed my hands to my face. My entire body shook as emotion poured out of me and a terrible coldness hit me right in the core.

Declan. Why? God, why?

Whatever trouble he was in, it shouldn't have come to this. I'd failed him. For him to see *this* as the only way out, I'd failed him terribly.

I had to call the authorities. There'd be questions, and I had no answers. Oh God, Sebastian. And Serena and Justin. What would I tell them?

As I stood, my eyes alighted on an envelope set on the bedside table on my side of the bed. I picked it up, recognizing

Declan's handwriting immediately. Tearing open the envelope, I removed the single sheet of paper and opened it.

I'm sorry. Forgive me.

That was it. No explanation as to why he'd decided to end his life. I dropped the paper, and it fluttered to the floor. Robotically, I stuttered into the living room to fetch my phone. It kept slipping through my fingers and took me three attempts to hold it properly. I dialed the emergency services and, in a voice that sounded nothing like me, told them what I'd found.

Sliding down the wall, I brought my knees up to my chest and hugged them.

Declan.

I struggled to wrap my head around it. If only I'd known how close to the edge he was, maybe I could have stopped him from...

Oh God.

The paramedics arrived a few minutes after my call. I answered the door in a daze, directing them to the bedroom. One of them stayed behind with me and kindly wrapped a throw around my shoulders while the other went to check on Declan. He returned a few moments later, grim faced.

"I'm sorry," the paramedic who'd stayed with me said as she read her colleague's bleak expression.

I nodded at her, waiting to feel something, anything, but my insides were numb, my eyes staring at nothing. So many people came and went; police, medical examiners, while I sat frozen in place and prayed this was all a terrible nightmare. Eventually, the paramedics brought Declan out on a stretcher, his body and face covered with a white sheet, and only then did the enormity of what had happened hit me. My knees shook, and I wrapped my arms around my stomach in an effort to hold myself together as I slowly came apart.

And then the guilt came, a tsunami of remorse that I hadn't gone to Declan's parents, or to Sebastian, with my suspicions that Declan had fallen in with a criminal gang, the debts he'd run up further evidence that he'd crawled into a very dark hole, one he chose to escape from with a finality that no one could save him from. Not me, not Serena or Justin. Not Sebastian.

They'd never forgive me, and I wouldn't forgive myself, either. I'd seen the signs, and I'd chosen to deal with them alone, not realizing that the consequences of that terrible decision would cost Declan his life. I'd asked for Sebastian's help too late.

Too late for Declan. Too late for me.

The police arrived and questioned me. I confessed about the debts but kept to myself my suspicions about drugs—or worse—criminal activity. I didn't want Declan's memory tainted or for the police to think of him as anything other than a victim of his own circumstances. The police officer offered to tell Declan's parents on my behalf, but I declined. Declan was my boyfriend—albeit in name only, given I'd slept on the couch for months—and therefore, the responsibility to tell his family lay firmly with me.

How I wished it didn't.

Hours later, the last of the authorities left, and I found myself alone, surrounded by a silence that threatened to swallow me whole. Acid burned in my stomach, and a swirl of emotions hit me all at once. Pain, grief, sorrow—and fury. A blind rage that crawled into my throat and caused a throbbing behind my eyes. Declan had created a horrific mess, and then checked out, leaving me to deal with it alone. To be the one to face his family and deliver the kind of terrible news no one should ever have to hear.

Immediately as those thoughts came to mind, a fresh wave of guilt washed over me. For Declan to choose to kill himself rather than face up to his problems meant he'd been in a far darker place than I'd ever imagined.

Why didn't you talk to me?

Another half hour passed where the same thoughts ran riot inside my mind. Over and over they chanted *why, why, why?* I'd never get the answers, and neither would his family, a dreadful truth we'd all have to live with for the rest of our lives. Unable to put it off any longer, I locked up the flat and trudged the short distance to the Tube station. I couldn't afford a cab after Declan had run up so much debt, and the thought of driving his car brought a lump to my throat. It would smell of him, although lately it smelled more of booze and cigarettes and weed. I didn't want to think about how I'd make rent this month or put food in my mouth, but fortunately I had enough money on my Oyster card to take the Underground. At least I'd still be able to get into work next week. Somehow I'd have to manage until my salary hit my bank account and then I'd have no choice other than to live off the increased overdraft Declan had arranged, slowly paying it back one month at a time until I got myself back in the black.

I shivered as I stood on the platform for the Tube that would stop closest to Serena and Justin's house, and then I changed my mind. Telling Sebastian and having him sit down with his mum and stepfather was a far better idea. Sebastian was stoic, calm, a man in control, and I needed that stable influence. It'd be hard enough to tell him the awful news, but to share the news with a mother that she'd lost one of her sons… no, I couldn't do it. And if that made me a coward, so be it.

I switched platforms.

The sight of Sebastian's enormous home set back on a leafy street in Holland Park brought fresh tears to my eyes. Declan's envy of his brother's success, and his multiple failed attempts to replicate them even on a minor level must be the reason he'd chosen a path of crime. It was the only thing that made any sense. How I wished he'd spoken to me, or to his family, rather than choose the path he had. Yes, he had a difficult relationship with his brother, but I had no doubts that Sebastian loved him and wanted to see him prosper. The brothers were so different. Declan lurched from one chaotic scheme to another in a pointless bid to compete with Sebastian, whereas Sebastian was measured, hardworking, and diligent. He executed to a plan, his success a sign of having a strategy and relentlessly pursuing it until it paid off.

If only Declan had had Sebastian's grit and determination.

If only Declan had been able to put aside his pride and baseless jealousy to ask his brother for help.

If only I hadn't stayed late at work finishing up some case notes.

I guessed that my life would be full of if onlys from now on.

Drawing on every ounce of courage, I walked up the stone steps toward Sebastian's front door and knocked twice. He might not be in, in which case, I'd have to camp on his doorstep for the second time in two weeks. There was a part of me that hoped he wasn't at home, or in bed fast asleep. At least then he could enjoy a few more hours of peace before his world ended.

A light came on in the hallway, and the door opened.

"Trinity?" Sebastian frowned. "What are you doing here so late? Is everything okay?"

I swallowed past an immovable lump in my throat. "I'm so sorry, Sebastian."

And then I promptly burst into tears.

7

Sebastian

I loved living in England, but the one downside? Winter. It's cold, dark, gray, and wet. Yet, as if Mother Nature realized me and my family needed a break, the morning of Declan's funeral greeted me with a dazzling blue sky, a crisp frost, and a distinct lack of the biting easterly wind so prevalent at this time of year.

I showered, dressed, and even made the guest bed in Mom's house, all of it on automatic pilot, a state I'd been in since the early hours of last Saturday morning. Whatever my problems with Declan—and there'd been many—I loved him. The finality of suicide, and the yawning absence of answers, was something I wouldn't wish on my worst enemy. The constant "whys" racing around my mind at all hours of the day and night had made sleep impossible to come by. The papery skin beneath my eyes looked gray and bruised, and I'd aged ten years overnight.

I passed Declan's childhood bedroom on the way downstairs, and just the sight of it caused a pain so sharp to rip through my chest that I had to brace one hand on the wall and wait for it to pass. I'd never pretend that we were close—I wouldn't disrespect him or me to suggest such a blatant lie—but now that he'd gone, and with his passing the chance for us to build the bridges I knew Mom had prayed for, guilt sat heavily on my shoulders, a constant reminder of how badly I'd failed him.

I hadn't seen Trinity since she'd dropped her bombshell early Saturday morning, stuttering out the dreadful news between racking sobs that had made her difficult to understand at times. On several occasions during the last week, I'd called to check on her, but she hadn't picked up the phone. I'd even left voicemails. She hadn't returned a single one, and try as I might not to take it personally, fresh waves of despair surged through me at her perceived rejection.

At one point, I'd driven by their apartment and parked a few yards away. I longed to be close to her, but a few minutes later, I'd berated myself for my actions and set off for home. Trinity had lost her boyfriend—who also happened to be my brother—and here I was, creeping past her home like some kind of weird stalker.

I hated myself for it, but I couldn't stop thinking about her, now more than ever. My focus should be on Declan, but my mind had other ideas. After today, she and I had no reason to see each other. I winced, a chasm opening up in my chest, the hole so big only one woman ever had a hope of filling it.

The one I'd never have.

The note Declan left behind told us nothing, gave none of his grieving family an ounce of peace or the answers we desperately sought to help us move on with our lives. I couldn't shake the feeling that Trinity knew more than she'd shared with me. Call it a sixth sense maybe, honed through working in the dog-eat-dog commercial world for all these years. I had a knack for sniffing out when details were being withheld, and however much she denied it, I believed that Trinity was hiding something. And after we'd gotten through the nightmare of today, I intended to find out precisely what.

Mom and Justin were in the kitchen when I arrived downstairs. I'd agreed to stay over last night, more for Mom's sake than my own, and as I took in her droopy eyes, downturned lips, and bowed shoulders, I knew I'd made the right decision. I held out my arms, and she almost fell into them. I caught Justin's worried frown. My stepfather and I had a challenging relationship, but one thing we could agree on was our concern for how Mom would cope with today. My mother wasn't a weak woman, far from it, but Declan was her baby, and although she'd never admit it, also her favorite. It still stung whenever I acknowledged that to myself, and Declan's death hadn't removed the throb of pain at that simple truth. I'd lost count of the number of times I'd almost had it out with her, but I'd backed away at the last minute. And now, I was glad that I had.

"Is Trinity coming here before...?" Mom trailed off, unable to utter the word "funeral". She leaned back, allowing me to look her in the eye.

"I'm not sure, Mom. She hasn't responded to my calls this week. Would you like me to try again?"

Mom shook her head. "If she isn't here when we have to leave, I'll assume she's meeting us there."

She extricated herself from my arms and stepped over to the stove, her need to keep busy clear.

"I hope you don't mind eggs for breakfast."

"Eggs are good, Mom."

∼

"The cars are here," I called through to the living room.

Mom rose stiffly from her favorite chair and, using Justin's arm for support and clutching her purse in her other hand, she joined me in the hallway. But when she got her first sight of Declan's coffin through the expansive clear windows on the hearse, and the word 'Son' spelled out in red and white roses, her knees went. Justin caught one side, and I caught the other.

"I've got you, Serena," Justin said softly, brushing his lips against her temple.

I averted my gaze, giving them their private moment. Mom and Justin's marriage had endured for a hell of a lot longer than hers and Dad's had, yet I still found it difficult to accept that my parents had divorced. Dad had offered to fly over to the UK when I called him to give him the awful news about Declan, but I urged him not to. Declan was Justin's son, and Dad being here struck me as completely inappropriate.

The three of us climbed into the back of the car and, sluggishly, we made our way through the grimy London streets to the crematorium six miles away from Mom's house. I stared out the window, Mom's hand curled inside my own, but I wasn't thinking about Declan. To my shame, all I could think about was Trinity and how she'd coped this last week. I yearned to see her, to satisfy myself that she was okay.

To offer her a shoulder to cry on—and pray that she took it.

I wasn't proud of myself and the feelings running riot inside me, but I couldn't deny them either.

The driver slowed the vehicle, stopping directly behind the car carrying Declan's coffin. I helped Mom out and scanned around, searching for Trinity. There was no sign of her. I crammed down disappointment and stood behind Mom while she spoke with the minister. After they'd finished talking, Justin took Mom's hand and together, the grieving parents walked into the church.

I followed on, alone. The entire ROGUES board had offered to fly to London to be with me, but I'd declined. They barely knew Declan, and while in my quieter moments, I admit the support would have been nice, I also didn't want to interrupt their lives for a service that would be over in less than a half hour. And besides, Upton and Belle deserved to enjoy their extended vacation, a trip to Rome added on after Upton proposed, and Belle accepted.

A few of Declan's friends that I recognized from his university years sat toward the back of the crematorium, and I nodded at them as I made my way toward the front pew. And then I saw her. Trinity. Head bowed, she sat on the left-hand side of the aisle. As we approached, she looked up and gave Mom a smile that barely held for a second. My heart clenched as her eyes turned to me, then quickly cut away. Mom went over and gave her a hug, whispering something in her ear that made Trinity nod. Justin kissed her cheek, then he and Mom sat on the right-hand side, leaving a space for me beside Trinity.

I sat, leaving as much room between us as the narrow pew allowed. "Are you okay?" I cursed the inadequacy of those words. Of course she wasn't okay. She'd lost her partner, the man she no doubt envisaged spending her entire life with.

"Are you?" she asked, ignoring my question and replacing it with one of her own.

"As well as can be expected."

I hated the formality of my response when what I really wanted to do was tell her that my heart was broken, not only because of losing Declan but also that now, I'd end up losing her, too. After the funeral and possibly one or two administrative things to clear up, Trinity Lane would walk out of my life, and I wasn't ready. I'd *never* be ready. Every time I'd seen her with Declan, I'd suffered another vicious cut to my heart, but this... this was a torment I wasn't strong enough to withstand.

"How's your mum?"

I shifted on the hard wooden seat and drowned in Trinity's golden-flecked eyes, so filled with pain and sorrow, and loss. "Heartbroken. I'm sure you can understand probably more than most."

"No one can understand a mother's love, unless you are one."

The minister began the service, and Trinity pulled her eyes from mine and faced the front. When the time came for the coffin to disappear behind the curtain, Mom's strangled sob reached me. She'd been so strong until now, but seeing her pain exacerbated my own, and I had to swallow several times to control my emotions. The last thing Mom needed was my pain and guilt on top of her own. I hadn't yet fully faced up to my culpability in Declan's terrible decision to end his own life. If I hadn't been so tough on him, or I'd worked harder to build up our relationship, maybe he'd have come to me in his time of need.

"Stop." Trinity's slim fingers, her nails painted a pale pink, wrapped around my hand. "Don't, Sebastian."

I should shake her off, but I was too lost, too selfish, and too hungry for any kind of physical connection that instead of drawing back, I tightened my hold.

"Stop what?"

"The guilt," she whispered. "It's written all over your face."

I looked at her then, truly looked at her, and reflected back at me was the guilt she spoke of, amplified to a power of ten. My instincts fired up, and the earlier thoughts of Trinity knowing more about Declan's decision to take his own life came roaring back.

"What do you know? Why did you ask me to come around to talk to him? What was going on with Declan?"

She bit her lip. "Sebastian, I—"

Mom's hand landed on my shoulder, cutting off our conversation.

"Trinity, darling, you're coming back to the house, aren't you? At least for a little while."

Trinity nodded sadly. "Of course, Serena."

"Then you must come in the car with us."

Mom slipped her arm through Justin's, and they made their way out of the crematorium. Trinity stood to follow them, but I stopped her.

"What do you know?" I repeated.

She tore her gaze away, fiddling with the strap on her purse. "I don't know what you mean."

"Trinity," I warned. "Talk to me, please. My brother is dead. Don't you think me and my family deserve answers?"

She repeatedly skimmed her teeth over her bottom lip, a sure sign of hesitation.

"I don't know why Declan killed himself, Sebastian. I wish I did."

"But you have your suspicions?"

Her eyes tracked my mom and Justin at the far end of the crematorium, chatting with a group of their closest friends.

"We should go. We don't want to keep your mum waiting."

She edged past me, and this time, I let her go. Now wasn't the time to push it, but Trinity's avoidance tactics had only served to further increase my curiosity. She knew far more than she was letting on, and one way or another, I'd uncover the truth.

8

Trinity

I avoided Sebastian by constantly staying on alert and tracking his every movement as he made the rounds of his parents' friends, and a few of Declan's old buddies from university. No doubt they'd have told Sebastian that they hadn't seen Declan in over a year—his 'new' friends made it clear they weren't welcome—which would create more questions for me. But as the wake drew to a close, and I said goodbye to Serena and Justin with promises to visit again soon, Sebastian appeared at my left shoulder, his grip on my elbow firm and uncompromising.

"I'll walk you out," he said, his tone brooking no argument.

"Thank you," I murmured politely.

Clouds had moved in during our time inside, chasing away the brilliant-blue sky from earlier, and a biting wind whipped around my ankles, and cut right through my coat. I tugged the scarf around the lower half of my face and buried my hands in my pockets.

"I should get going."

"I'll drive you home," Sebastian said.

I shook my head. The last thing I needed was more time alone with him. More time he'd use, no doubt, to grill me about what I knew. Which actually wasn't much. Just suspicions and conjecture without foundation.

"I'd rather you didn't," I said. "I'd prefer to be on my own."

I turned away, hating my stiff, unfriendly attitude when what I really wanted to do was throw myself into his warm embrace and never leave.

"What do you know about my brother's suicide? And don't say nothing. That's disrespectful to me and to my brother's memory."

I flinched at such directness. "I'm not feeling great," I lied, shooting him a quick glance over my shoulder. "Can we do this another time?"

His lips flattened, and he gave me a curt nod. "Very well. I'll come by first thing in the morning."

I nodded glumly. At least I had a brief stay of execution. I wasn't being obstructive on purpose, but when I shared what I knew about Declan's drug habit and what I suspected in relation to his dealing drugs, it'd show Declan in a terrible light to a brother who already had a low opinion of him, and that broke something inside me.

"See you tomorrow."

The Tube was quiet, unsurprising given rush hour was still a couple of hours away. I flopped into a seat and closed my eyes, wishing I were a better actress. I should have refuted Sebastian's firm questioning at the crematorium, convinced him that Declan's death was a tragedy, no more, no less. But he'd seen something that had set off his inner curiosity, and a man like Sebastian Devereaux was used to getting answers. He'd know all the techniques to eke out every crumb of truth. I didn't stand a chance.

Greeted by a thick blanket of clouds as I emerged from the Underground a ten-minute walk from my house, I lowered my head and plowed through the strong easterly wind. I scurried into a long, narrow alleyway that connected two side streets, increasing my pace in a bid to get to the other side as fast as possible. I hated this shortcut, but without it, my journey time from the Underground station to my house more than doubled.

I jumped at a clanging sound in one of the tiny backyards. Spooked, I broke into a run. A guy appeared from the other end, walking toward me, a knitted hat pulled low over his eyes. My heart thudded, prickles racing along the back of my neck. I made space for him to pass. When he did, I let out a huge, relieved breath.

Stop being an idiot, Trinity.

I'd walked this route hundreds of times, and while the dimly lit streets and narrow alleyways gave me the jitters, lots of people used the same means to get around.

Another guy came into view, the glow of a cigarette visible in the muted light. He took a long drag, blowing out a cloud of smoke as he strolled in my direction. And then he stopped. Right in front of me.

I froze, my feet rooted to the spot. "Excuse me. Can I get past, please?"

He didn't move, just continued to puff on his smoke, his hooded eyes raking over me. Blood drained from my face, my heart drilling against my ribcage, and despite the freezing temperatures, my hands grew clammy. Fear had a smell, and the evil curve to this guy's lips told me he'd smelled mine.

"What do you want?" I asked in a voice that sounded nothing like me.

A hand landed on my shoulder, spinning me around. I screamed. The guy who'd walked past me a few seconds ago held a knife to my throat while the second man wrapped a thick forearm across my abdomen.

"Scream again and I'll cut you. Where are they?"

I blinked rapidly, my mouth parting. I swallowed, then licked my lips. "Wh-where's what?"

"Don't play dumb. He must have told you what he did with them."

The arm across my stomach tightened, and the man who had a hold of me fisted a clump of my hair, yanking hard. My scalp burned, and I cried out.

"Better tell him, love. He ain't someone to mess with."

"I don't know what you're talking about," I croaked.

The guy in front of me pressed the tip of the knife into my throat. "The guns. Where has Declan stashed the guns?"

Horror froze in my chest, his words seeping through my fear-soaked brain.

Declan, what have you done?

Adrenaline flooded my system, pumping and beating in a desperate attempt to break free. My body urged me to flee at the same time as my legs locked in place. The man's face blurred. For the first time in my life, I faced the possibility of death.

"I don't know anything about any guns."

"Don't lie to me!"

I flinched, craning away from the blade, the steel glinting in the darkness. My tongue stuck to the roof of my dry mouth. I swallowed again. "I'm not! Declan never told me anything. I didn't know he was dealing guns."

"Not dealing, darlin'. *Stealing.* Your boyfriend stole a shipment of guns from me, and I want them back."

"I-I don't know where they are. You have to believe me."

The two men locked eyes, silently conversing. The one standing in front of me dropped his arm. Free of the knife at my throat, suppressed air forcibly expelled from my lungs, and my entire body slumped forward.

He rubbed his smooth chin, his eyes glinting in a way that

churned my stomach. "Then I guess there's only one thing you can do. Find them."

"How? I don't even know where to look."

He grabbed my face, pinching his thumb and forefingers into my cheeks. "Smart girl like you can figure it out, I'm sure. And if you don't..." He leered at me and jerked his chin at his friend. "I'll let him deal with you. You won't be the first woman he's fucked to death. He ruts like a dog."

A vile snigger sounded behind me, and nausea swirled in my stomach.

"I can give you a preview if you like, darlin'." He rubbed his erection against me.

Don't respond. Stay quiet. Breathe.

"You have two days," the one with the knife said. "And don't do something stupid like call the cops. If you do, I'll end you, and I'll take my time doing it, too."

He leaned in and licked my face. I held myself rock-still and closed my eyes, opening them only when I heard fading laughter from the two men.

Somehow, I made it home. My legs gave way the second I stumbled through the front door. Scrambling to my feet, I twisted the deadlock and slotted the chain into its housing, then let my knees go from under me again.

A choked cry forced its way into my throat. *Guns?* How had Declan become embroiled in something so serious? Guns were such an alien concept. Hell, our police didn't even carry firearms, unless they were guarding the airport, or part of an armed response team. Unlike some other countries in the world, gun crime was still a rare occurrence in Britain. The idea of Declan touching, holding, maybe even firing a gun sent an icy shiver running through me. And now, I had to find out where he'd hidden a bunch of them. In two days.

I hadn't a clue where to begin.

My entire life was crumbling around my ears, and there

wasn't a damn thing I could do to stop it. Up to my eyeballs in debt, no money to buy food or pay rent, and now threats of physical harm, even death, if I didn't locate the stolen guns.

I had no other choice. It was time to tell Sebastian everything.

I navigated to my contacts and located Sebastian's details. Taking a deep breath, I made the call.

9

Sebastian

I crawled up Trinity's street, searching for a parking space, but it was jam-packed on both sides, leaving only a one-car width space to drive. If anyone came in the opposite direction, one of us would have to reverse. I eventually found a gap in the parked cars a couple of streets over, squeezing my Merc in between an aging Ford and a powerful motorbike.

The pavement was icy as I strode the short distance to Trinity's apartment. During the entire journey south of the river, I'd replayed her plea to see me tonight over and over. She'd tried to hide it, but the tremble in her voice and the rapid way she spoke—very unlike her usual composed manner—set my mind racing in all kinds of directions. She'd left my parents' place less than two hours ago, her reticence to talk to me clear. What had changed? We'd arranged to speak tomorrow anyway, so it must be something important for her to change her mind that rapidly.

I rapped on the door. A shuffle came from inside.

"Who is it?"

"Sebastian."

"Hang on."

The lock clicked and the chain rattled, and then Trinity opened the door. I took one look at her, and my chest filled with apprehension. Her skin was pale and clammy, and she appeared jittery. No, not jittery. Terrified.

"What's the matter?" I demanded, stepping inside the apartment and closing the door behind me. I glanced around. Horror hit me squarely in the gut. I'd never been inside their place. Nor had Mom or Justin as far as I was aware. On the rare occasion I'd heard her mention popping around, Declan had made a bullshit excuse and steered the conversation in a different direction. And he'd made it abundantly clear that Hell would freeze over before he'd welcome me into his home, and —God help me—I hadn't pushed it.

I should have fucking pushed it.

A small patch of damp darkened one corner of the compact living room, the black spores ominous and a goddamn health hazard. The wallpaper had started to peel, and the whole place had a musty odor.

Bad enough that my brother had lived here, but Trinity?

Seb, you fucking asshole.

I rubbed my hands over my arms. "Jesus, Trinity, It's like an icebox in here. Why haven't you put the heat on?"

She pulled a throw tighter around her shoulders, and her whole body seemed to curl in on itself. "I can't afford the bills."

My throat constricted. What the hell was going on? What kind of man was I that this had been going on right under my nose and yet I'd remained oblivious?

"Don't worry about that now." *Or ever.* "Let's get this place heated. Where's the boiler?"

She pointed to an archway on the other side of the living room. "It's in the kitchen."

I strode over. The kitchen was marginally better than the living room, but not by much. I fired up the boiler, then plugged in the electric kettle and flicked it on.

"I'll make some tea," I called through to Trinity.

"There's no milk," she said.

I frowned. No milk. No heat. No money for bills. A prickle crept across the back of my neck. I opened the fridge.

Fuck.

Apart from a tiny piece of cheese and one slice of ham, plus the usual assortment of condiments, there wasn't a damn thing to eat.

I turned off the kettle and the heat and strode back into the living room.

"Pack a bag, Trinity. You're coming to stay with me."

Her eyes widened. "I-I can't."

"You can, and you will. You are *not* staying here. Now pack enough things for a few days, or I'll do it for you."

She lifted her fear-filled golden eyes to me, and something pulled tight inside my chest. She looked so vulnerable, and that concerned me more than anything. Trinity wasn't the vulnerable kind. She wasn't one of those ball-busting women either, but she had a quiet strength that drew people to her.

"I hate dragging you into this, Sebastian, but I don't know what else to do."

She covered her face with her hands, and her shoulders shook. Torn between putting my arms around her—which was *not* a good idea—and doing something practical, I sensibly chose the latter.

"Stay here. I'll toss a few things in a bag, take you back to my place, and then you can tell me what's going on. Nothing's unfixable, Trinity."

She dropped her hands into her lap where they sat listlessly. "I wish that were true."

I ignored her comment—there'd be plenty of time for questions later—and crossed to the only other door off the living room, which I guessed was the bedroom. I averted my gaze from the bed and opened the closet. The sight of Declan's clothes hanging from the rail yanked on my heartstrings. I stared at them for a few moments, touching one or two items. What a waste of a life. Goddammit, I should have tried harder with him, forced him to accept my help. If I had, he'd still be alive today.

And you wouldn't stand a chance with Trinity.

Filled with self-reproach for even thinking something so inappropriate, I dragged my gaze away from Declan's gear and reached up to the top shelf for a sports bag. I threw in a couple of pairs of jeans, some T-shirts and sweaters, and two pairs of sneakers. The hardest part was opening Trinity's underwear drawer. I closed my eyes and grabbed a few handfuls of the items, then stuffed them into the bag along with her toothbrush and a few toiletries from the bathroom. If anything was missing, I could easily come back, or buy her whatever she needed.

I zipped up the bag and returned to the living room. In my absence, Trinity had put on her coat, a positive sign she'd given in to my demand that she return to my home with me. It couldn't be easy for her. In truth, we hardly knew each other, even if I spent far too many hours dreaming of what it would be like to hold her and kiss her and take her to my bed.

"Ready?"

"Yes."

"I parked my car a couple of streets over. Do you want to wait here while I go get it?"

"No," she said, far too quickly. "I'd rather come with you."

"Then let's go. Got your keys?"

"Yes."

She further worried me on the walk to my car when she kept looking over her shoulder, almost as if she expected someone to jump out of the bushes and attack us. And when I got her settled in the passenger seat and eased away from the curb, the way her shoulders lowered and she blew out a slow breath through tightly pursed lips fired up my instincts. Between leaving my mom's house and this moment right here, something awful had happened to her. One thing I'd learned about Trinity was that pressing her got me nowhere. She'd tell me what was wrong in her own time, and I'd have to bite my tongue until she felt ready.

I noticed her shivering and increased the heat. She shot me a wan smile and wrapped her arms around her body as if she was trying to hold the broken pieces of herself together. I left her to her thoughts while I navigated the busy London streets. Rush hour had descended, and there were busses and taxis and too many goddamn cyclists who seemed intent on causing a nasty accident by weaving in and out of the traffic and leaving the hazard perception to others.

Gliding the car into my personal parking spot at the front of the house, I cut the engine and got out, reaching into the back seat for Trinity's bag. She joined me on the sidewalk, and I motioned to her to go on ahead. She trudged up the stone steps and waited by the door while I opened it. I took her coat and hung it on the stand inside the hallway, then led the way to the smallest sitting room and the one I preferred at this time of year because of the log burner that pumped out welcome heat, greatly needed in the middle of an English winter.

"Would you like a drink? Something to eat?" She'd eaten at Declan's wake, so that was something, but given the lack of food at her place, I couldn't help wondering whether that had been the most she'd eaten in a while.

"Tea would be lovely if you have some," she replied.

I ground my teeth at her formal response, almost as if she were attending an interview. Then again, what did I expect? I'd kept out of Declan's way as much as possible, just as he'd kept out of mine. Trinity and I hardly knew each other, and I got the distinct impression she'd rather keep it that way. That she'd called and asked to see me must've cost her dearly, especially given how I'd left things earlier today. She must know I intended to drill her for answers on what she knew about Declan's suicide. But that could wait for now. I was much more interested in why she'd left my mom's house a short time ago with a clear intention to put as much space between me and her as possible, only to phone me two hours later and beg for me to go by her apartment.

"Have a seat. I'll be right back."

I made a pot of tea—an English custom that I'd grown fond of—and carried the tray back to the sitting room. I poured her a cup and left her to add milk and sugar as she preferred. She chose neither. When she let the silence linger and seemed intent on studying her cup of black tea rather than open up, I kicked off the conversation.

"Please tell me what the matter is."

She lifted bleak eyes to mine. "Declan was in a lot of trouble, Sebastian. And now, so am I."

Prickles of anxiety crept along the back of my neck, down my arms, ending with tingles in my fingertips. I flexed my hands to avoid the onset of pins and needles.

"What kind of trouble?"

"The worst kind."

She peeled her gaze away from mine and stared at the flames flickering behind the glass window of the log burner.

"On my way home tonight, two men accosted me."

My tongue suddenly felt thick inside my mouth, and my heart began racing, my mind jumping to all kinds of horrific conclusions.

"What men?" I croaked.

Please, please, God, don't let them have raped her.

"One of them had a knife. He held it to my throat while the other one grabbed on to me from behind."

As horror sat on my chest, she scrubbed her hands over her face, and only then did she look at me.

"They told me that Declan had stolen some guns and if I didn't find them and give them back, they'd... they'd... oh God, Sebastian, what do I do? I don't know anything about any guns. I can't... I can't..."

Sensing an approaching panic attack, I gripped her hand and squeezed. "Breathe, Trinity. Take deep breaths for me."

My mind scrambled as I tried to put the chaotic thoughts into some semblance of order. Men with knives. Guns. Trinity threatened. I fought to process it all. What the *fuck* had Declan gotten himself into? And with whom?

"I'm calling the police."

"No!" Trinity exclaimed, panic spilling across her face in an instant. "You can't. They said they'd kill me if I called the police. And besides, you'd have to tell them about Declan's part in this, and it'd kill your mum to know what he'd become."

I wasn't convinced, but I nodded, letting it lie for now until she'd told me the entire story. And then I'd decide on the best course of action. If Mom had to face up to Declan's faults in order to save Trinity, then so be it. We had already lost one life to this fuckup of a situation. I refused to lose Trinity as well.

"What else did they say?"

"Nothing. Only that I have to tell them where the guns are and that I had two days to find them." Her bottom lip trembled. "I don't want to die."

"You're not going to die." I rose to my feet and kneeled, removing the cup of tea from her. I set it down on a table, then wrapped her small, chilly hands in mine. "I won't let anything happen to you. Promise."

I refrained from adding that I'd kill every last bastard who harmed a single hair on her head, and if Declan were still alive,

I'd kill him, too. Guns? What the fuck? How had he gotten embroiled in something so dangerous?

"If I don't find the guns, then you won't be able to stop them. You can't be with me every second of every day."

"Want to bet on that?" I smiled reassuringly, even though I felt very differently on the inside. I was a businessman, not a criminal mastermind. But I had two things in my favor: money, and the blinding love I had for this woman. Not that I could ever tell her how I felt. A confession like that coming on the heels of Declan's death and this latest appalling development was the very last thing she needed to hear.

"There's more," she said.

And then it all spilled out. How she'd had concerns about the company Declan was keeping, the all-nighters he and his friends pulled, filled with drugs and booze, his mood swings and temper tantrums, her fears that he wasn't only using drugs, but dealing them, too. And finally, the debts he'd run up.

"I can't buy food, let alone make rent. I got paid today, but all that's done is covered a fraction of the overdraft. I just don't know what to do."

At last. A problem that was within my gift to solve. "Don't worry about the money. I'll take care of it."

She rubbed absently at her arms. "I can't let you do that. It's my debt and I'll settle it."

Proud, stubborn woman. I admired her grit, but she wouldn't win this argument. "It's Declan's debt, not yours, and therefore, it's my debt. I will fix everything, okay?"

She lowered her head and nodded. "Okay."

"Hey." I clipped her under the chin. "You're safe here. I'll never let anything happen to you."

A faint smile touched her lips, but it fell before I had time to savor it. "Did I know him at all?"

I hitched up a shoulder. "Seems like neither of us did."

She released a long sigh and, resting her head against the

back of the chair, she closed her eyes. "I don't think I'll ever trust anyone again."

My chest constricted, and something inside me died.

"Let's get you up to bed. Everything will seem better after a good night's sleep."

I took her bag upstairs to the same room she'd stayed in the night of Elliot and Sage's wedding and left her to get some rest. Returning to the sitting room, I poured a large brandy and flopped into the chair she'd vacated, relishing the warmth from her body still present in the fabric. Slowly, the enormity of the mess Declan had left behind hit me. Given the brevity of the suicide note he'd left, we'd never know the truth behind his decision to take his own life, but if I were to hazard a guess, I'd say he felt he had nowhere to turn.

I'd failed my brother, and I'd carry that awful truth with me for the rest of my life.

10

TRINITY

Clanging noises came from the direction of the kitchen as I made my way downstairs the following morning. Surprisingly, I'd fallen asleep the second my head hit the pillow, and I hadn't woken once during the night. Sebastian's parting comment about things seeming brighter in the morning proved itself true. I hadn't shaken the bone-chilling fear of having a knife held to my throat and my life threatened—and I doubted I ever would—but I no longer felt the imminent threat of danger that I had back at my flat. Having Sebastian close by gave me an unerring feeling of safety, and while the things I told him about Declan last night must have come as a hell of a shock, he hadn't criticized me once for not informing him of my suspicions sooner. Not that I'd have blamed him if he had. I was culpable. If I'd told him or Serena earlier, maybe I could have avoided this terrible tragedy, and Declan would still be alive.

I paused, one hand on the wall, waiting for the wave of guilt to pass. Once the lightheadedness receded, I carried on down the stairs.

"Morning," I said shyly as I entered the kitchen.

Sebastian glanced over his shoulder from his position at the stove. He hit me with a brilliant smile that I had no idea what I'd done to earn.

"Morning. How did you sleep?"

"Well, thank you."

He tapped the wooden spoon against the pan, then set it down on a piece of kitchen paper. "Tea or coffee?"

"I can do it."

He motioned with his arm. "Nonsense. You're a guest."

"Tea then, please."

I slid onto one of the chairs at the breakfast bar and watched him move around the kitchen, completely at home and comfortable in his surroundings. Not that he shouldn't be, but I couldn't help thinking it odd that a billionaire business mogul made his own breakfast. For some reason the thought made me giggle which, given what happened yesterday, it surprised me that I still had the ability to find humor in situations.

"What's so funny?" Sebastian asked, hitting me with another one of those amazing smiles as he slid a mug of tea over to me.

Why hadn't I noticed before that he had such a beautiful smile? Or how gorgeous he was?

A blush crept up my neck, and I hastily picked up my mug to hide it. "I thought someone of your stature would have a housekeeper or something."

He quirked an eyebrow. "Someone of my stature? Hmm, sounds a bit pompous. Is that how you see me?"

"God no," I rushed to say, and then I caught the glint in his eye and I cocked my head to the side. "You're teasing me."

He rested his elbows on the breakfast bar and propped his

palms under his chin, and something about his stance caused my insides to flip. I'd always had a bit of a crush on Declan's elder brother, a kind of stricken awe at how in control he was—the complete opposite to Declan—and now, I'd begun to see Sebastian in a completely different light. And that worried me, not least because I was damned sure he didn't see me as anything other than his dead brother's girlfriend.

Once again, the jaws of guilt gnawed at me. We only buried Declan yesterday, and already I was having inappropriate thoughts about his brother. What kind of woman was I? My hankerings to belong might have entailed staying with Declan long after I should have ended things between us, but that did not mean it would *ever* be right to think about his brother in a non-platonic way.

"I'm only teasing to take your mind off everything," Sebastian said.

I blinked, realizing I'd zoned out, and forced a smile. "It worked."

Sebastian straightened. "How are you feeling, though? Honestly?"

"Better than I was. I'm still struggling to process it all. So much has happened." I sipped my tea. "How am I going to find those guns?"

"Wrong question," he said. "How are *we* going to find those guns? And the answer is, we're not." He reached into the back pocket of his jeans and slid a business card across to me. "He is."

I picked it up. "A private investigator?"

"Yes. He comes highly recommended." He lifted the cuff of his white shirt and checked his watch. "He'll be here in half an hour."

For the first time since those men had threatened me in that dark, dank alleyway, a spark of hope filled my chest. "Do you really think he can?"

His forehead puckered. "There aren't any guarantees, but his credentials are extremely impressive."

"So you're not going to call the police?"

"Not yet. Let's give him a few days and see what he uncovers and then, if necessary, we can adjust the strategy. Like you said, if we involve law enforcement then it'll all come out about Declan, and I'd rather keep my mother's memories of him intact, if at all possible. But if your safety is at risk at any time, I'll call the police immediately."

I glanced down at the business card again. "I don't have a few days. They're going to come for me tomorrow."

"Then we buy ourselves some time. We let the private eye do his job while we put some distance between you and them."

I frowned. "What do you mean?"

He grinned. "Have you ever been to Scotland?"

∼

"I am *not* getting in that death trap."

Sebastian laughed. "It's the quickest way to get to my estate. It's pretty remote."

"Can't we drive or get the train?"

He rolled his eyes. "I can reel off the safety statistics of my helicopter versus Britain's road and rail network if you like, but if we want to get there before dark, we need to get going."

I eyed him suspiciously. "And you have a license for this thing?"

"Thing?" He stared at me in mock horror, his palm pressed to his chest. "I'm offended. This isn't a 'thing'. It's a highly technological piece of equipment that'll get us to my place in less than two and a half hours."

"That long?" I squeaked.

Sebastian opened the door and motioned for me to get inside. "The more you procrastinate, the longer it'll take."

Reluctantly, I climbed up into the glass bubble. Once I was inside, my nerves jangled, far worse than when I'd had my feet on solid ground. Sebastian got in beside me and jerked his chin at a pair of huge, padded headphones hanging from a hook to my left.

"Put those on and fasten your belt."

I clipped the seat belt in place and fixed the headphones over my ears, jumping when Sebastian's voice came through them.

"Ready?"

"No."

He laughed again.

The blades started up, the whirring gradually getting louder. Sebastian spoke into the radio, but none of what he said made sense. I sat on my hands to stop myself from doing something stupid like trying to bail out, but when the machine lifted into the air then tilted forward, to my shame, I screamed.

"You're okay," Sebastian said confidently.

"How do you know?" I hit back.

His responding chuckle warmed my insides, a delicious heat circling low in my abdomen. As we rose higher, and the ground fell away, my heart rate finally slowed to a more normal rhythm. The view from up here was spectacular, and as we left the sprawl of London behind, England's beautiful scenery came into its own, a patchwork of greens and browns. The farther north we traveled, the more a blanket of pristine snow covered the green landscape.

"Will there be snow at your place?"

"Yeah. Tons of the stuff. It's in the middle of nowhere."

"How come you bought a house so remote?"

He glanced over at me. "It helps me to think."

"About what?" I asked, genuinely interested in his reply.

He seemed to consider my question for a while, poking his

tongue into the side of his cheek and tipping his head to the side.

"There's a lot of demands on my time, and, occasionally, I just need to get away and allow myself the head space to mull over things. Scotland is the perfect place to do that, as you'll soon see. It's incredibly peaceful, and I hope you'll be able to relax there. It's probably the safest place I can take you."

"Why?"

"There's nothing around for miles. Only one road in and out, and the nearest village is ten miles away. But that's not why it's so safe."

"Why then?"

He flashed a grin. "You'll see."

I waited for him to expand, but when I realized he wasn't going to share any more details, I pouted. "Fine. Have your secrets."

He snickered. "If the wind changes, you'll stick like that."

I laughed, too. Before the awful events of the last few days, I'd hardly spent any time with Declan's brother, and none where it had been just the two of us. Now that I had, I grappled with how different they were. At least if I used the last twelve months as a comparison. Before that, Declan still smiled, although not nearly as often as his elder brother seemed to enjoy doing. His warm personality and take-charge attitude, not to mention his dove-gray eyes, aristocratic jaw, and blade-sharp cheekbones made for one very attractive man.

There you go again. Just stop.

But as much as I ordered my brain to only think platonic thoughts when it came to Sebastian, it seemed determined to defy me. It wouldn't surprise me if the trauma had caught up with me and pushed everything out of alignment somehow. I'd had several shocks in a row, and no one knew how they'd react to adversity until faced with it. Yeah, that was probably it. Sebastian's kindness and inclination to help me and take care of everything meant my brain had confused gratitude with something more.

I hoped the private detective worked fast and found what those men were searching for. I was on compassionate leave from work for another week, but after that, I'd have no choice other than to return. And that scared the hell out of me. The only escape from those men was to somehow locate the guns Declan had stolen and return them. I could only hope that was enough, and they didn't seek further retribution.

"You've gone awfully quiet," Sebastian's voice sounded in my ears.

I twisted in his direction. "Just thinking?"

A weird expression crossed his face, but before I took a closer look, the shutters came down.

"About Declan?"

No, about you.

"What if your private detective doesn't find those missing guns?"

"He will," Sebastian said confidently. "And if he doesn't, we move to Plan B."

"Which is?"

"We go to the police."

"It'll kill your mum."

"She'll survive. She's a strong woman. And we won't have a choice. We can't run for the rest of our lives."

I couldn't help noticing he used the word 'we' an awful lot, and while my stomach fluttered at the thought of Sebastian and I being in this together, it was only a turn of phrase. He didn't mean it literally.

I worried my bottom lip. "Do you miss him?"

Sebastian did that tongue poking thing again, which he seemed to do every time he was thinking hard.

"Don't think badly of me, but no, I don't. Me and Declan were about as far apart as brothers could be. My friends are more like brothers to me than Declan ever was. I loved him, and I always will. He is—was—family, and that will never change. But it's hard to miss someone you never really knew, and that's proven even more true with the latest revelations." He pressed a couple of buttons overhead and banked slightly to the left. "I blame myself for our estrangement. I should have done more to encourage him. Instead, I berated him and expected him to be more like me. He wasn't me. He was him. And if I'd cut him some slack, then maybe he'd have felt more able to come to me for help when he needed it the most."

His blunt honesty took me aback, and it must have shown on my face because he pulled his lips to one side and shrugged.

"You must miss him terribly."

I took a few seconds to answer. It was imperative that I got this right. "I miss the Declan I first met, but the man he became over the last year? No, I don't miss him at all. I'm devastated that he felt suicide was his only way out of the mess he'd created, and, like you, I wished he'd reached out for help, but the man I once loved left me a long time ago. I've grieved for him already."

Sebastian's eyebrows shot north, his incredulous stare evidence that my confession had come out of the blue.

"I'm sorry," he finally said.

"So am I."

We flew on in silence, with Sebastian only breaking the lull in conversation to draw my attention to the odd landmark. The weather drew in, the sky above growing heavy with snow. A few flakes splattered the windscreen.

"Can you fly in the snow?"

"Flying, yes. Makes landing a little trickier from a visibility standpoint, but we'll be there in about ten minutes, so hopefully we'll get her on the ground before the worst of the weather hits."

I wrung my hands and bounced my legs, and prayed Sebastian's piloting skills were up to the challenge. "I've never been all that keen on the word 'hopefully.'"

He spared me a glance, took in my restless legs, then refocused his attention on the business of flying. "I've landed in far worse conditions if that makes you feel any better."

"I'll feel better when my feet are back on planet Earth."

Lucky for me, the snow didn't get any worse, and a few minutes later, Sebastian pointed to a large dwelling surrounded by a thick blanket of snow.

"That's my place."

I craned my neck to get a better look. "I don't see the road you mentioned."

"It's there, buried under all the snow. Scotland's had quite the dumping of the stuff."

He banked around the back of the house to where a large area had been cleared for him to land. I furrowed my brow.

"Is someone here?"

He nodded. "My caretaker, Jack. He lives here year-round. See that building next to the barn? That's Jack's home."

"Wow, he must get lonely up here all by himself."

"Not at all. He prefers the isolation. And besides, the village isn't far away, so he's not completely cut off from civilization."

He flicked a few more buttons and lined up ready to land. A few minutes later, we hit the ground with a bump.

"And... down."

I blew out a hugely relieved sigh. "No one is happier than me."

He cut the engine, and the noise abated as the blades slowed.

"Come on. Let's get you inside. And then I'll introduce you to Jack, and to your personal bodyguard."

I widened my eyes. "Bodyguard? You said I was safe up here. Why would I need a bodyguard?"

Sebastian grinned. "Ah, but this is no ordinary bodyguard. He's the reason I brought you here."

He opened his door and jumped down onto the untouched snow.

Bodyguard? Today got weirder by the minute.

11

Sebastian

"Jack, great to see you." I strode forward and shook the hand of my caretaker, simultaneously clapping him on the upper arm. "Thanks for getting everything ready at such short notice."

"Not a problem, laddie," Jack said, his usual form of address bringing a smile to my face. Jack was only about five years older than me. "And is this the wee bonnie lass you told me about?"

"Yes." I beckoned to Trinity, who'd decided to loiter just inside the door. "This is Trinity Lane, a friend of mine. Trinity, this is Jack. He takes care of everything around here."

"Nice to meet you, Jack."

"Aye, and you, lassie. No need to stand over there in the draft. I got a fire burning and a pan of soup on the stove."

Right at that moment, Boomer, Jack's German Shepherd, came bounding in, his fur damp from being outside. Trinity jumped almost out of her skin and let out a squeal as the enormous dog launched at me, nearly pushing me over.

I laughed and ruffled his head. "Boomer, is that any way to greet me." I gripped him firmly by the collar. "Sit."

He immediately plopped his ass on the kitchen floor and, tongue lolling out the side of his mouth, gazed up at me with adoring big brown eyes.

"Trinity, meet Boomer. Your bodyguard," I added with a laugh.

She peeked at the dog, then me, glanced briefly across at Jack, then returned her attention to Boomer, who lived up to his name by letting out the loudest bark in greeting, the deep sound echoing off the thick stone walls.

"He's... terrifying," she said as Boomer rolled back his lips, showing an enormous set of fangs.

"Nah, he's a pussycat," I said. "Come and say hello. I promise he's harmless."

"Then how will he make a good bodyguard?"

I grinned at her savvy comment. "He's a pussycat... with us. If any strangers set foot on the property, though, that's when Boomer earns his keep."

Her eyes darted to Boomer again, a little wild, a lot apprehensive. "I'm a stranger."

"Trinity, for Christ's sake, come and say hello to the dog. And then you won't be a stranger."

She looked as if she'd rather stick her hand in the roaring fire burning in the grate than pet Boomer but, after a couple of seconds' delay, she padded forward and gingerly petted the top of his head.

"There you are. You're fine."

"I'm not a big fan of dogs," she admitted. "I don't mind the small ones but... I mean, have you seen his teeth?"

I laughed, and even Jack snickered. "I promise you're completely safe."

Boomer barked again, then licked the back of her hand.

"See, best of friends."

Trinity didn't appear at all convinced, but she did pet him for a second time, which was progress at least.

"I'll leave you to get settled. Boomer," Jack barked, cocking his head at the panting dog. Boomer bounded after him, his claws clicking against the stone tile. Wind whistled through the house as Jack wrenched open the back door. He slammed it behind him, leaving Trinity and I alone.

She seemed a bit lost and definitely looked tired. I shrugged out of my coat and hung it on a coat rack right inside the door.

"How about a bowl of Jack's soup, and then I'll show you to your room and let you get some rest? We can do the grand tour tomorrow."

"That sounds lovely."

She placed her coat next to mine. I motioned for her to sit at the kitchen table while I set out soup bowls and filled them with the hearty chicken broth. I cut a few slices of bread, too. I gave her a bowl, put one on my side of the table, and placed the stack of bread between us.

"You survived the flight," I said, dipping a hunk of bread into the soup.

Trinity followed my lead. "Only just. I'm not keen to repeat the experience."

"And there was me thinking I'd converted you."

She shook her head. "Not a chance."

I grinned and let a comfortable silence descend while we ate. Trinity didn't seem to need to fill quiet moments with inane chatter, and neither did I. Another thing we had in common.

I thought back to what she'd said during the flight regarding her relationship with Declan. I'd made an assumption they were happy, but if what she told me was true, I'd surmised incorrectly. On the rare occasions I'd seen them together, they'd appeared content, but then again, no one knew what went on inside a relationship. Not that their troubles meant anything for us. There *was* no us. There could never *be* an us. Even if their relationship had died a long time ago, that didn't make it appropriate for me to make a move. She'd always be my brother's girlfriend. Even if that wasn't true, Trinity showed absolutely no signs of any kind of attraction toward me. No furtive looks or coy blushes or fluttering eyelashes. Not a single indication of even mild flirting.

"Do you know, you do this thing with your tongue when you're chewing over something."

My head came up, and I frowned. "Huh?"

"You poke your tongue into the side of your cheek, and sometimes, your head bends to the right when you're lost inside your thoughts. Your eyes kind of glaze over, too."

Funny, no one had ever mentioned that to me in my entire life.

"Is that so?" I mused.

"It is."

She helped herself to another slice of bread and tore off a piece. It pleased me she was eating.

"What were you thinking about?"

I cleared my throat. "Nothing important." I finished my soup, then stood and took my bowl over to the dishwasher, stacking it inside.

Trinity polished off the last of her meal, and no more questions about my woolgathering were forthcoming.

"Jack makes a great soup," she announced.

"You should taste his rabbit stew. It's legendary around these parts."

"Here's hoping I get to sample it."

She yawned and stretched, and my eyes slipped south to her round, full breasts. My jeans suddenly felt too tight, and I turned my back, both as a way to stop my unwarranted staring, and in case Trinity saw the clear outline of my erection. So far, I'd curbed any physical reactions to her, but out here, in the middle of nowhere, just the two of us, I seemed to have lost all semblance of self-control.

I palmed the back of my neck, shame a boulder in my stomach. Declan's death had changed nothing. To act on my feelings for Trinity would be a betrayal of his memory. Caught between intrinsic loyalty and a hunger that only grew stronger, I snatched up our bags. I had to get out of here before I risked revealing the truth.

"I'll show you where you're sleeping, and then I'll leave you to unpack."

Without waiting for her to agree, I strode out of the kitchen. She followed on behind, and I led her up the stairs and to my favorite guest room in this house. It overlooked the mountains that curved around the rear of the property, and on a sunny day, it was a marvelous sight. Not that she'd see it tonight, but hopefully she'd wake to the view in the morning, providing a blizzard or a dense fog that often blighted this part of the world in winter didn't arrive and spoil it.

I put her bag on the floor and studiously avoided eyeballing the bed or her. "There's a bathroom through there," I pointed to a door in the corner, "and the remote control for the TV is on the dresser in case you want to watch Netflix or something. I'm at the other end of the hall if you need anything. It's early, but it's been a long day."

She yawned for a second time, covering her mouth with her hand. "It sure has."

I paused on the threshold, then, finding my head empty of words, I dipped my chin and left her alone. I unpacked the clothes I'd brought, enough for a few days, by which time I hoped the private investigator would have located the guns and both Trinity and I could put this behind us.

And then what?

Would we simply return to our lives, go our separate ways,

or would this experience bind us together? And if it did, what did that mean for both our futures? The old cliché that absence made the heart grow fonder had certainly proved true in my case, but now, thrust into this situation and forced to hole up here as a way to keep Trinity safe from the criminal gang Declan had stolen from, I had the awful feeling that I'd only end up falling deeper in love with a woman who'd never be mine.

Despite what I'd said to Trinity about turning in early, I was far too wired to sleep. Instead of changing for bed and climbing underneath the covers, I wandered back downstairs and poured a glass of whisky that Jack's father distilled at his farm. Before buying a place up here a few years ago, I hadn't liked whisky all that much, but Jack had converted me. Then again, there was a vast difference between the mass-produced, bitter whiskys found on supermarket shelves and the smooth, amber liquid that Jack's dad manufactured, a lifetime of experience behind him.

I pulled the chair closer to the fire and sat, staring into the flames, the yellow and golden flares reminding me of Trinity's eyes.

God, Trinity...

I set down the glass, closed my eyes, unfastened my jeans, and dipped my hand inside. The second I gripped my dick, a loud groan fell from my lips. Until now, I'd avoided jacking off to Trinity's image, although I'd been tempted plenty of times, but it always felt... oh, I don't know... disrespectful, maybe. To both Trinity and Declan. And it probably still was, but after spending all that time in an enclosed space where the smell of her, so sweet and fresh, had filled my nostrils, coupled with the sight of her perfectly round tits straining against her T-shirt when she'd stretched a few minutes ago, my self-control snapped.

I pumped harder, imagining Trinity's full, rosy lips wrapped around the head of my dick, her luminous eyes looking up at me as she sucked me deeper inside her mouth. The sounds of pleasure reverberating deep in her throat. Her velvety-soft tongue...

"Ah, shit."

I snatched a bunch of tissues from a box on the table beside me with seconds to spare. Tossing the used tissues into the fire, I shoved my dick back into my pants and let my head sink back against the chair. I'd hoped a fast orgasm might've eased the ache in my gut, but instead, it had worsened. I longed for Trinity. I *burned* for her. I wished I didn't. God, how I wished I didn't. My life would be a lot easier if I found an available woman to obsess over, but at the age of thirty-four I knew my own mind—and my heart.

Basically, I was fucked.

I knocked back the remains of the whisky and trudged upstairs to bed. I hovered outside Trinity's room. I even pressed my palm to the ancient oak wood, as if that somehow brought us closer together. And then I told myself I was being a jerk.

Even so, it took every ounce of my self-discipline to walk away.

12

Trinity

I threw back the curtains and beamed at the sight greeting me. There wasn't a cloud in the sky, and the sun peeked over the top of an enormous mountain range, the bright rays glinting off the snow-covered slopes. This was my first ever visit to Scotland, and given the stunning view, I questioned why it had taken me so long when it was only a few hours by car or train from London.

Or two and a half hours in a helicopter flown by your dead boyfriend's beautiful, sexy, and charismatic billionaire brother.

I closed my eyes and let my mind drift to Sebastian. I shouldn't. It was completely wrong on so many levels to have the kinds of intimate thoughts I'd started having about him, but I couldn't help it. Maybe it was the risk of imminent danger that had brought into sharp focus the sheer beauty of the man, both on the outside *and* on the inside. His sense of humor and light-hearted teasing made him easy to be around, and his kindness toward me—especially as we'd only met a handful of times before the horrible events of the last couple of weeks—continued to amaze me. He had every right to lay blame at my door, at least in part, for Declan's death. For the rest of my life, I'd wonder whether I could have saved him if I'd involved his family at an earlier stage or whether, as I'd worried, it would have pushed Declan and me apart even further than we'd already traveled.

I guess the answer would always remain a mystery.

The guest bathroom was bigger than the bedroom in my flat, with a huge walk-in shower, twin sinks, and a large picture window that showed off those glorious mountains. And the normally frosted glass window, prevalent in bathrooms, was absent. I could strip naked and no one would see me.

Correction, Jack might, but if I had my bearings right, the annex Sebastian pointed out last night that doubled up as Jack's home was on the other side of the house.

Even so, I drew the blind. Wasn't worth chancing it.

I switched on the shower, and in seconds, steam rose from within the stall. I stripped off my PJs and stepped underneath the spray. Hanging my head, I let the water flood over my back. I must have stood like that for a couple of minutes, relishing the hot needles, the peace and quiet, and the sense of relief that I was a long way from London, far from where those men could get their hands on me.

Every time I thought about how they'd cornered me in that dank, smelly alleyway, and how powerless they'd made me feel, I wanted to punch something.

No, not something. I wanted to punch Declan for being so bloody stupid.

I might never forgive myself for keeping my suspicions from his family until it was too late, but I also doubted whether I'd forgive Declan for leaving me at the mercy of those thugs.

Squeezing a dollop of my vanilla and peach shampoo onto my palm, I lathered my hair, digging my fingertips right into my skull. I rinsed, conditioned, then stepped onto the bathmat and wrapped a towel around my head and another underneath my armpits. I brushed my teeth, then rooted around in a set of drawers for a hairdryer. I found one in the bottom drawer and plugged it in. It took an age to dry my too-thick hair. Bored, and with aching arms, I gave up halfway through and tied it into a ponytail. It'd soon dry.

I dressed in jeans and a jumper and shoved my feet into a pair of slippers that Sebastian had thankfully packed on my behalf. I hated walking around in bare feet and didn't want to wear my tennis shoes all day either. As I walked downstairs, I pondered what I'd do all day, stuck out here in the middle of nowhere. I was certain Sebastian wouldn't want me hanging around him the entire time. When he put all our things into his car yesterday before we'd driven out to where he kept the helicopter, I noticed him specifically pack his laptop. That meant he planned to work while he was babysitting me, although I did wonder whether he'd get reception up here. That thought made me check my phone. Full signal? Wow. Impressive. I couldn't even get that sometimes in the center of London. He must have paid to have some kind of booster signal installed, at a considerable price no doubt. Then again, billionaires didn't find money a limiting factor like the rest of us mere mortals.

I found the kitchen by retracing my steps from last night. It was empty, but the fire still burned in the grate—or more likely had been freshly lit this morning—pouring out so much heat that I rolled up the sleeves on my jumper and thought about returning upstairs for a T-shirt. On top of the stove sat one of those old-fashioned kettles, the kind that whistled when they reached boiling point. I filled it with water from the tap and, after fiddling about for ages, got the stove to light. Investigations of several cupboards eventually revealed a box of tea bags, and I rinsed a used cup that I found in the sink.

"Finding your way about okay, I see."

I jumped and spun around, my hand pressed to my chest. "Jesus."

Sebastian grinned. "Sorry, didn't mean to startle you."

I narrowed my eyes, peering at him. "You have very silent feet."

"All the better for sneaking up on people," he said, his smile broadening.

I got the clear impression that he enjoyed teasing me—and I enjoyed being on the receiving end. Not that I planned to admit that to him anytime soon. If I did, I'd lay odds on him doing it more, and all that would do was pull me further under his spell.

"How did you sleep?"

"Like a log," I said. "And that view? I almost couldn't tear myself away."

"Yeah, it's pretty special."

He opened one of the few cupboards I hadn't explored and took out a mug, placing it next to mine. Grabbing a pot of coffee, he filled it almost to the brim, then added a dash of milk.

"We haven't brought you over to the dark side then?" I asked, jerking my chin at his choice of drink versus mine.

"I don't mind tea, once in a while, but if I drink too much, Homeland Security might not let me back into America."

His eyes twinkled as he said it, and I caught myself just in time before he noticed me staring. I could drown in his eyes and die happy. I shook my head of such thoughts and made the leap to a safe subject.

"Do you plan to? Return, I mean."

He lifted his left shoulder. "One day. Maybe. I like living in England, and I adore being so close to Europe. There's a lot of Americans who'd love to be in my position. Plus, my mom's here, and me being so close has allowed us to repair our relationship, to some degree anyway."

I remembered Declan telling me that Sebastian's parents split when he was only a toddler, and his mum had left him in the States with his dad. He hadn't mentioned a difficult relationship, though.

"You must have missed her when she moved to England."

His lips twisted to the side. "My dad did a great job playing both parts. Mom made her choice."

Catching the bitter tone to his voice, I struggled for what to say to a comment like that. The kettle saved me by letting out a high-pitched whistle. Sebastian killed the heat and poured boiling water over my tea bag.

"Sorry. Too much information."

"Not at all," I said. "Believe me, I know what it's like to feel abandoned."

He arched a brow. "Oh?"

From his surprised response, I surmised that Declan mustn't have told him about my background.

"My parents were killed in a fifteen-car pile-up on the motorway shortly before my tenth birthday. I grew up in the system." I shrugged in pretense that it didn't hurt like hell, even though, almost two decades later, it still did. "That's a fun ride."

"God, I'm sorry." He raked a hand through his hair. "I must sound like a complete twat, moaning when I have nothing to moan about."

A smile inched across my face. "Such a British curse word sounds funny in your American accent."

"It's one of my favorites," he admitted with a grin. "You Brits have so many to choose from. Bollocks is another favorite of mine."

"Yeah, we're all about the swearing."

He blew across the top of his coffee, his warm gray eyes locked on mine. I almost squirmed, a reaction to the mass of butterflies that had chosen this moment to make their presence felt. Inside

Sebastian's kitchen, the silence seemed to stretch forever, and breathing became a gift I couldn't seem to master. And right when I thought I may die from lack of oxygen, Sebastian broke the spell.

"I thought you might like to take a walk this morning. There are a few great hikes we can do straight from the house that aren't too strenuous, and the views are to die for."

I hid a welcome gasp of air behind a fake yawn. "I'd love to, but I don't have boots or a warm coat."

"You do now." He reached underneath the kitchen table and hoisted up a large bag. "I had them delivered this morning."

I dove inside the bag and removed a thick, padded coat, a pair of stout boots, gloves, a bobble hat in a shocking pink and —kill me now—thermal underwear. A speedy glance at the labels told me the clothing was in my size.

"How on earth…"

"I know the right people," he said.

I lifted my wrist and checked my watch. "We arrived late yesterday, and it's only eight-thirty in the morning, and you've already figured out my size *and* had the clothing delivered."

He held his arms out to the side, palms up. "What can I say. I'm a miracle worker."

"You certainly appear to be," I murmured, more to myself than him. "I can't afford to pay for these."

He fired a ferocious glare in my direction. "Please tell me you don't actually think I'd take a single penny, even if you could afford it? You're my guest here, and these are gifts."

I realized then that the one thing Declan and Sebastian had in common, despite their many differences, was a fierce sense of pride, and I'd stomped all over his. But I had my pride, too, and Sebastian had already offered to clear the debts that Declan had run up with the bank and the credit card company. I could square that away under the heading of 'family,' but this was different, and even to my untrained eye, the coat and boots hadn't come cheap.

"I didn't mean to insinuate anything or hurt your feelings. It's hard for me to accept such—generosity."

I'd almost said charity, and if I had, I imagined Sebastian's glower might deepen. As it was, his brow smoothed, and he dipped his chin in a barely there acknowledgement of my point of view.

"I understand. Maybe look at it a different way. Without the right attire, I'd have to go walking by myself, and that would make me miserable."

He faked a pout, and I stuttered a laugh.

"If my mother had lived, she'd have had a name for you. An imp." *And Dad would have probably gone with dangerous, especially as, with every passing second, I was falling deeper and deeper under Sebastian's spell.*

"Aren't imps adorable?"

"No," I replied. "They're annoying."

His wide grin and sparkling eyes gave me a feeling of weightlessness, and my fingertips tingled with the urge to explore his smooth face, his broad shoulders. His taut chest and flat, hard stomach.

"Then there's work for me to do. Before the day is out, I'll have you eating out of the palm of my hand."

I forced a smile. If only he knew. I already was.

13

SEBASTIAN

Trinity insisted on clearing away the breakfast dishes, and while I objected at first, in the end, I let her go ahead. I got the impression that she wanted to stay busy to keep her mind off her troubles, most, if not all, caused by Declan.

My eyes tracked her around the kitchen, taking in every goddamn faultless inch of her, from the flawlessness of her skin to the way her waist nipped in at the sides. From the curve of her ass to tits that I didn't have to touch to know they'd fit my hands perfectly. I could sit here and pretend, hide behind a sense of obligation in riding to her rescue, but deep down, I knew the truth. By coming to me and asking for my help, she'd opened the door to my greatest fantasy: to spend one-on-one time with the woman who'd haunted my dreams for over two years.

I intended to relish every second—until the time came when I had to let her go. And it would. As soon as the investigator I'd hired located those guns, she'd have no reason to hole up here with me. We'd return to London, hand over the weapons, and that could very well be the last time I ever saw her.

I *hated* the thought.

"You look miles away."

I blinked. "Sorry?"

"And you're doing that thing with your tongue again."

I suppressed a groan. Every time she mentioned my tongue, I had to swallow the urge to show her what I could *really* do with it. Clearing my throat, I pushed back my chair and stood. "Want to head on out?"

"That's something else I've noticed," she said, ignoring my suggestion that we get going on our walk.

I folded my arms over my chest and inclined my head. "Go on. I'll bite."

Her lips formed the smallest, most secretive smile I'd so far seen painted there.

"You deflect."

Aware of exactly what she meant, I nonetheless pretended otherwise. "Deflect what?"

She arched both eyebrows and mirrored my stance by crossing her arms, too. "I should imagine it works rather well in the boardroom. Not that I'm experienced in such tactics, but I can guess that's how the mechanics of big business operates."

Beautiful and astute, too. Then again, in her line of work, she must know how to tell if someone was telling lies. I went with a sliver of the truth. To give her just enough to put her off the scent of what really went on in my mind whenever she was nearby.

"I was thinking about you, if you must know."

She appeared flustered at my response, her hands moving jerkily as she lifted one of them and rubbed the back of her neck. Probably mortified that she crossed my mind in any capacity.

"What about me?"

I wished I could be completely honest, but I intuitively knew that if she ever found out how I truly felt about her—how I'd *always* felt about her since the day we met—it would horrify her. And I wouldn't blame her for that reaction. There were romances that some might frown upon, and others that were downright wrong. Unfortunately for me, Trinity and I fell into the latter. Even if the day came when she might join me on the same page—a highly unlikely event—I doubted Mom would accept us as a couple. And she wouldn't be the only one. We'd face disapproving looks and whispers behind our backs wherever we went, and I refused to put Trinity through that.

Jesus, will you listen to yourself? I appeared destined to keep falling down these rabbit holes, where I fantasized that Trinity was attracted to me. And it was not only stupid but foolish, since she hadn't given me any signs.

"Just how it'll do you good to keep busy until we can return to London and you can rid yourself of me."

I flashed a grin.

Trinity simply gave me a blank stare. And then she nodded. "Yes, that will be nice."

She turned away and therefore missed the way I flinched at her cavalier response to what I'd intended as a joke, but she'd taken literally, allowing her to share what she really thought of this enforced situation. It backed up the correct decision I'd made never to share my true feelings. A masochist I was not, and I didn't intend to be.

She pulled out a chair opposite and tugged on her boots, bending to tie the laces. I did the same, glad that she still wanted to take a walk. We slipped on our coats and gloves, and Trinity crammed a woolen hat over her hair. When she looked up at me and grinned, her eyes shining in eagerness to get going, I breathed a sigh of relief that she'd decided not to make things awkward between us. Or maybe she'd figured out I had been joking after all. Whatever her reasons, the tension biting across my shoulders disappeared, replaced with a rush of happiness. I never thought the day would come where I'd get to bring Trinity here, to a place I'd grown to love, and take her hiking in the mountains, something I adored doing whenever I got the chance. Yet here we were, and I was going to make the most of every second.

I opened the kitchen door, and a blast of cold air swept in, and with it a few flurries of snow. But the clear blue sky indicated an absence of a fresh downfall, backed up by the weather forecast I'd checked this morning. The weather up here had a habit of closing in fast, and while I knew these trails almost by heart, if we ended up in a blizzard, even I might have trouble leading us back down again. People died on mountains in Scotland every single year, and I didn't intend to add either of us to that awful statistic.

The snow crunched beneath our feet as I led the way around the back of the house and out toward the footpath that slowly snaked upward. The depth of the snow made it tough going, and after ten minutes, both of us were panting.

"We sound like a bad porn movie," Trinity said, and then she gasped and slammed a hand over her mouth. "Oh God, I'm sorry. That was completely inappropriate."

I burst out laughing, more at her chagrin than her comment, although both were equally amusing. "I can't say I'm familiar with the subject."

She snorted. "Oh, come on. Isn't it a rite of passage for all teenage boys to watch at least one?"

"That particular rule must have passed me by."

"Oh."

"You sound surprised."

She shrugged. "I guess I assumed it was the done thing for boys."

"And not for girls?"

Another shrug. "I didn't have real friends growing up. Maybe if I had, my answer, and my experience would be different."

I cursed underneath my breath. I knew nothing about the UK social care system, nor the US one come to think of it, but I could hazard a guess that forging meaningful relationships wouldn't be easy in an institution where someone might be there one day and gone the next. Adopted, fostered, or moved to another facility in a different part of the country.

"And no one ever adopted you?"

She forced a smile. "No. Too old. Everyone wants the cute babies or adorable toddlers. A damaged ten-year-old who refused to speak for an entire year after her parents died wasn't up there on the list of 'must haves.'"

She spoke matter-of-factly, but the truth of her pain lay in her eyes. *A whole year without saying a word to anyone.* Jesus.

I folded my hand around hers and squeezed her fingers through her gloves. Meant as an act of friendship, a kind gesture toward someone hurting, it nevertheless set off all kinds of reactions inside me, not the least of which was an erection as hard as the rock and granite towering above us.

"I'm so very sorry."

"It was a long time ago."

Her tone was flat, devoid of emotion, yet spoke volumes about unresolved issues that would one day come back to haunt her if she didn't confront them. I held her gaze for a second or two, then tore my eyes away and fixed my attention on the incline of the path ahead of us.

"Shall we carry on before our feet freeze?"

"Sounds good."

It took us another hour to reach the summit, most of it traveled in silence. Several times I'd gone to speak, more to break the ice than because of a need to share something, but each time I'd glanced over at Trinity, the firm set of her jaw and determined, fixed stare had deterred me. But when we got to the top and the view of the valley on the other side opened out in front of us, she perked up considerably, a gasp of astonishment falling from her lips.

"Oh, Sebastian. It's wonderful."

She ran to the other side, peering over the edge where the rock fell away far more steeply than the side we'd climbed. And then she just stood there, hands on her hips, staring at the point where the sun cast half the mountain range in light with the other side remaining in darkness.

I sidled up beside her. The sun emphasized the highlights in her hair, and the brisk wind had brought much needed color to her cheeks. There was so much I wanted to say, most of it poetically pathetic, all of it inappropriate and positively unwelcome. And so I remained quiet and tried to enjoy this moment for what it was, even if it pained me to do so.

"Sebastian?"

I looked down at her. "Yes?"

"Why have you never settled down?"

My eyes widened at the left-field question. "Um— I." I grimaced. "That's a bit personal, isn't it?"

She winced, and I felt like a complete jerk.

Tell her the truth.

"Sorry, forget I asked."

"No, I'm sorry. It's just..." *Fuck.* "I never found the right girl." *Liar.* "Actually, that's not true. I found the right girl but it... it didn't work out."

The liberation of telling her at least a partial truth rushed through me, but when she tipped back her head and I saw pity swirling in her eyes, my jaw locked, and I twisted away and put a few feet between us.

"Sebastian."

Her palm landed on my back, and I almost leaped into the

air. Three layers of clothing between us and still I got an electric shock from her touch.

"We should get moving. It might take us longer to get down depending on how agile you are on your feet."

I strode off, pausing after a few feet to make sure Trinity was following on behind. I waited for her to catch up, then set off again. We didn't share another word on the descent, nor when we arrived back at the house. But as I unlaced my boots, Trinity broke the impasse.

"I'm sorry. I didn't mean to make things awkward between us. Your private life is none of my business."

I stared at her, blinking, groping around for the right words, none of which came to mind. Not acceptable words anyway.

"I'll leave you alone," she said when I continued to say precisely nothing in response to her apology—one she had absolutely no need to make.

Expelling a resigned sigh, she spun on her heel and left me sitting there nursing a head full of regrets and a heart filled with sorrow.

14

Trinity

I stayed out of Sebastian's way for the rest of the day, sneaking down to grab an apple when I glanced out of my window and saw him talking to Jack. For hours I'd reflected on the woman who'd stolen Sebastian's heart, wondering what had gone wrong, whose fault it had been, and whether there was a chance of a reconciliation.

I clenched my teeth at the sudden pain lancing my stomach. I wasn't sure when exactly it had happened, but there'd been a shift inside me, one that made me wish for more from a man I had no right to demand a single thing from.

But as the sky grew dark and night fell, my growling stomach forced me to leave the confines of my room and return downstairs. I entered the kitchen and found it empty. I wasn't sure whether the feeling that rushed through me was one of relief or disappointment. I cocked my ears, listening for sounds of life, but apart from the loud ticking of a clock on the wall, I could have been completely alone. Maybe I *was* alone. A shiver ran down my spine at the thought, but I immediately discarded it. I might have pissed off Sebastian with questioning that had brought up painful memories, but he'd never desert me without at least telling me first.

I made myself a cheese sandwich and dragged out a chair at the kitchen table to eat. This place was so different from Sebastian's contemporary home in London, and although he hadn't yet given me the tour he promised when we arrived last night, I expected the rest of the house would follow in a similar traditional vein.

I cleaned up the crumbs and rinsed my plate in the sink, then sighed, wishing I'd brought my e-reader, or at least a book. Alone and with only my thoughts to occupy me, I grew restless, pacing up and down and chewing on my fingernails.

"Oh, screw it."

I strode down the hall, but instead of going straight upstairs, I systematically poked my head inside every door on this level. I found the living room and stared longingly at the real fire, unlit right now, but I could imagine cozy nights curled up on the squishy couch, watching the flames flicker and dance. I also came across a formal dining room, a little snug that had a window seat overlooking the mountains at the back of the house, and a downstairs cloakroom. On the other side of the stairs, kind of hidden away at the end, was another door, but unlike the others that had been ajar, this one was firmly shut. I pressed my ear to the thick mahogany wood, listening for any signs that Sebastian might be inside. Nothing. Not a sound. I gripped the brass doorknob and twisted it.

"Oh. I'm sorry."

Sebastian glanced up from his place behind a huge antique desk, one of those that had a green leather top, the old-fashioned piece of furniture in direct contrast to the sleek silver laptop that had Sebastian's full attention. Well, it had until I'd burst in unannounced.

Questioning gray eyes bored into mine, and his right eyebrow quirked up at the edge.

"You okay?"

I nodded, the tight sensation in my chest receding now he hadn't ordered me to get out. "Are you?"

He pulled his lips to one side and pushed back his chair, his hands moving from the keyboard to rest in his lap. "A little embarrassed if truth be told."

I frowned. "Embarrassed? Why?"

"Because my behavior obviously made you feel as if you had to hole up in your room all day."

"I thought you might appreciate some time alone."

"Alone time is the very last thing I want." He rose to his feet and stretched out his back. "Look, how about this? Give me a half hour to finish up a couple things, and then I'll cook dinner, light a fire, and download a movie—your choice."

Heat developed between my thighs at the idea of curling up next to Sebastian where I could pretend, for a few hours at least, that I'd met him first, and the last few weeks never happened. That we were boyfriend and girlfriend who'd escaped to their beautiful cottage in the Scottish Highlands for a dirty weekend away from the hustle and bustle and grime of London.

And then I woke myself up. Figuratively speaking. Only a few hours ago, I'd pushed Sebastian into admitting that he'd once loved someone, evidently very deeply, and now I was having these stupid fantasies about me and him. Not to mention he was Declan's brother. Nothing would—*could*—ever happen between us.

"Trinity? You still in there? You kinda zoned out on me."

I blinked rapidly and forced a bright smile. "Sorry. Just stunned with the idea of a man cooking me a meal."

He bought my cover-up of an excuse, throwing back his head and laughing heartily.

"Bachelor, remember. I either learned how to cook or lived on takeout food."

"You could hire a chef."

"Not my style. As I mentioned to you the other day, I don't even have a housekeeper, just a cleaner who comes in twice a week. I prefer my privacy."

Yeah, I could see that about him. He had enough money to have staff catering to his every whim if he chose to. But despite the houses and the helicopter, there was something very humble about the man standing before me. And that in itself was hellishly attractive. He didn't flaunt his wealth, and given I was poorer than a church mouse, I appreciated that more than I'd ever be able to convey.

"Can I help with any preparation for dinner?"

"No. You go and relax, and I'll be out shortly."

"Okay."

I left him alone and returned to the living room. Sitting on the couch, I shut my eyes and allowed myself a brief fantasy, one where Sebastian lit a roaring fire, slowly peeled off every item of my clothing, lay me down on the thick rug in front of the hearth, and, with the heat from the flames licking at our naked bodies, slowly made love to me.

I lost track of time, engrossed in the labyrinth of my vivid imagination. The slam of a door jerked me back to reality. Flushed and needy from my unfulfilled daydream, I made my way to the kitchen. Finding it empty, I about-turned, but at the sound of approaching footsteps, I pulled out a chair and sat at the table. Sebastian appeared a few moments later. He broke into a smile, one that did all sorts of pleasurable things to my insides and made my already needy clit pulse and throb.

"There you are. Right, shall I start dinner?"

"Only if you let me help," I said.

He arched a brow. "And if I don't, you'll go hungry?"

My lips curved into a smile. I adored how he teased me, yet another thing that made him so very different from Declan. Even before he'd started bringing his 'new' friends home, he'd suffered black moods. Maybe in the very beginning, we'd laughed and joked with each other, although my recollection of the start of our relationship was hazy, expunged by the much more prevalent and horrendous recent memories.

"Yes."

He chuckled, then opened a drawer and removed a potato peeler. He set it on a chopping board and grabbed a brown paper bag that was filled with potatoes. "They'll need washing first. Jack only picked them today."

I filled the sink with water and proceeded to scrub the mud off the skins. "You grow potatoes in this weather?" I jerked my chin toward the window, although it was far too dark to see outside.

"*I* don't grow anything." He laughed and waved his hands in the air. "These are not green fingers. But Jack grows a lot of fruit and vegetables all year round. It keeps him busy, and he enjoys it. But to answer your question, these particular potatoes weren't grown outside. He also has a small greenhouse that I had built for him a couple of years ago during an especially cold winter."

I inclined my head. "You're a good man, Sebastian."

I swore he blushed, but he looked the other way, hiding whatever color had bloomed in his cheeks. "We're all made up of good and bad. I'm no saint. None of us are."

"Still, you did a nice thing, and I wanted to tell you that."

His chin dipped briefly in acknowledgement, and then his beaming smile made a comeback. "Stop procrastinating and peel."

I giggled and followed his orders. We fell into a comfortable silence, and it wasn't long before we sat down to a hearty meal of steak, boiled potatoes soaked in butter and flavored with parsley, and a pile of steamed green vegetables that Sebastian told me Jack had also grown right here on his property.

"There must be a lot that goes to waste considering Jack is here by himself for a lot of the time," I said as I stabbed my fork into a potato and slipped it into my mouth. "Oh God, that's so creamy. Nothing like you get in the supermarket back home."

"It's because they're fresh," Sebastian explained. "And no, there's no waste. Jack packs the excess food into boxes and delivers them to the elderly folk in the village."

"How thoughtful."

"We all have to do our bit to help communities thrive and prosper."

I chewed thoughtfully. It was as if Sebastian had given me a pair of glasses that helped me see the world differently. My upbringing, tough early adult years where I tried to make something of my life, and then meeting Declan and all the shit he brought to my door had given me a cynical edge, made me think that there was only pain and suffering in the world. My choice of career hadn't helped alter that world viewpoint either, but sitting here with this man who did so many good things for others, maybe there was hope for humankind after all.

"Have you heard anything from the private detective?" I expected little, especially as Sebastian had only met with him yesterday morning before we flew up here. God, had it only been a day?

"Not yet. He said he'll send in regular reports. Try not to worry. It's very early days."

"Yeah, I guess."

He reached over the table and squeezed my arm, and I almost launched out of my chair at the bolt of electricity that shot up my arm. Lucky for me, I remained seated. Explaining a reaction like that wouldn't be fun.

"It'll be okay, Trinity. I promise. One way or another, I'll make this go away."

I looked into his earnest gray eyes, darker in the dim light of the kitchen, and I believed him.

15

Sebastian

As Trinity put away the last of the dishes, I forced a ball of hope back into the box where it belonged. Being together like this, doing mundane shit such as clearing away after dinner, felt so fucking right, yet everything about it was wrong. Or at least *society* would say it was wrong. The question I had to answer was whether I gave a flying fuck about societal rules, or if I believed my happiness was important enough to reach out and grab the one thing I wanted more than anything else in the world, and screw the consequences.

It wasn't even as if they'd married or had kids. And she'd freely admitted they'd been having problems for quite a while before Declan took his own life.

"Why didn't you leave Declan?" I asked, kneeling in front of the fire to light the kindling. "If you were unhappy, I mean?"

At the heaviness in her sigh, I glanced over my shoulder and winced at the pained expression on her face, the drooped mouth, the way she stared at her feet with a glassy look in her eyes.

"Initially, I believed I had the skills to help him. I should have been able to help him, but everything I tried just made things worse." She heaved another deep breath. "And I was scared."

Her voice came out so small and barely audible that I stopped what I was doing and sat beside her. I took her hand in mine, ready to release her if she showed the slightest sign she didn't appreciate the gesture. As it was, she curled her fingers and gripped on to me tightly.

"Scared of what?"

She chewed her bottom lip and shrugged. "Of being alone, I guess."

Her eyes darted to mine, then immediately diverted back to the floor.

"I stayed far longer than I should have." She laughed bitterly. "I mean, we weren't even a couple at the end. I stopped being his girlfriend months ago when I moved to sleep on the sofa. I told him it was either the drugs or our relationship. He made his choice."

Another bitter laugh spilled from her lips while I reeled from the revelation that they weren't sleeping together. *Jesus Christ.* They weren't fucking sleeping together.

"When you've spent years hoping and praying for a family after a tragedy cruelly ripped yours away, you grab on to the slightest sign you might have found what you've been looking for."

I blinked, forcing myself to pay attention to her even as my mind spun at a hundred miles an hour.

"Yeah, I guess," I rasped.

"And even when that dream turns into a nightmare, you still keep hoping that you're wrong and everything will turn out the way it was supposed to. Instead, that decision could very well cost me my life."

I released her hand and applied the gentlest pressure to her chin, easing her around to face me. "I'm sorry Declan let you down, but *I* won't."

That didn't even come close to what I really wanted to say, but if I told her how I felt, and how *I* could be the family she so desired, she'd run a mile. But when her eyes softened, and she pressed her hand to mine, I almost caved.

"You're too kind, Sebastian. Thank you for being my friend."

And just like that, the hope of more shattered into a million pieces.

Fuck. The dreaded friend zone.

I forced a smile. "Anytime. Now, how about that movie?"

∽

The credits rolled at the end of the movie, and I exaggerated a groan. "That was quite possibly the worst film I've ever had to sit through."

"Oh, stop." Trinity swatted my arm. "You don't fool me. I saw you swipe away a tear when the heroine died."

I gave her my best astonished stare. "I did not."

She giggled. "Don't lie to me, Sebastian Devereaux. I know what I saw."

"Oh, yeah?" I tickled her side, and she squealed, scrambling out of my reach.

"Tickles? I take it all back. You're a wicked man."

I chuckled and went in for a second attempt. She twisted away, then clambered to her feet, laughing hard, her hands held out in front of her.

"No tickling!"

I pretended to consider her request, then grinned. "No deal."

As she read my intention, she made a dash for the door. I caught up to her easily and went in for the kill. Almost hysterical laughter burst from her, and she doubled over, squirming and shrieking. And then I remembered who she was and who I was.

Horrified, I stopped what I was doing and took a step back. I blinked several times and licked dry lips, my chest heaving from both exertion and desire, neither of which I had a right to. Not with Trinity.

"Sebastian?"

I showed her my back, then strode over to the fireplace and rested my hand on the mantel.

"I'm sorry. That was… inappropriate."

She joined me, and although I felt her gaze on my face, I kept my attention fixed on the glowing embers in the grate.

"What was inappropriate? Having some much needed fun?"

I looked at her then, at her flushed cheeks and wide eyes filled with confusion, and my heart just broke. Until this moment, I hadn't thought there was anything left of it to break. Turned out I didn't know jack. Why the fuck did I have to fall for the forbidden fruit?

"It's late. We should turn in for the night. I have a busy workday tomorrow. If you like, I can ask Jack to take you into the village rather than being stuck here all day by yourself. There's a small bookshop that has a café on site if you're interested."

Her eyebrows raised. "It's nine-thirty. Hardly late. And I'm happy to get out of your way if that's what you need, but…"

I waited for her to finish her thought. It never came.

"But what?" I asked, too curious to let it lie.

"Tell me what I did wrong."

My lips parted, and I shook my head. "You did nothing wrong."

"Then explain why you think what you did was inappropriate."

"Because you were once Declan's girlfriend. And you're inside my fucking head!" I spun away and raked a hand through my hair. "Fuck."

The room filled with silence, and for a second, I thought she might've left. And then she came to stand beside me. I noticed how she kept her distance. Couldn't blame her. The idea of me lusting after her had probably horrified her. Christ, if she knew the kinds of dreams I had, and what I'd like to do to her, she'd take her chances with the gang in London rather than spend another second in my company.

"Sebastian, look at me."

"It's probably best that I don't."

"And why is that?"

I studiously kept my eyes off her face. I should rip out my tongue, too. What a fucking idiot to open this particular box. There was no going back now, no avoiding her constant questions. It didn't mean I had to answer them, but for Christ's sake, I could kick my own ass right now.

"Sebastian."

She laced her tone with a firm command, a demand that I give in and obey. I continued staring into the dying embers of the fire. She huffed and then inserted herself between me and the fireplace. And still I didn't dare meet her gaze.

The pads of her fingers softly traced my jaw, and my breath caught in my throat.

"What are you doing?" Hell, was that me? My voice sounded like I'd smoked twenty high-tar cigarettes, one after the other.

She raised herself up onto her tiptoes, but that still left her several inches shorter than me. Cupping both her hands around my face, she softly pressed her lips to mine. The kiss lasted less than a second yet rendered me paralyzed.

"Is that okay?" she asked.

I couldn't speak, only nod.

She smiled. "And this?" Again, she kissed me, this one a touch longer.

"You're killing me," I ground out.

"Then take control," she whispered.

I groaned. *God forgive me. And God help her.*

I threaded my fingers through her sun-kissed hair, tilted back her head, and just stared at her. She took my breath away, and I wanted to kiss her more than I wanted to fill my lungs with air. But at the same time, we'd only ever have one first kiss—those fluttering pecks she initiated didn't count—and I wanted her to remember this moment for the rest of her life. Whatever happened from here on in, *this* had to be a memory to last a lifetime, for both of us.

She stared at me in wide-eyed surprise, those rosy lips parted in expectation. And still I refused to give in to the desire burning in my veins. Sometimes anticipation far outweighed reality, and if it held true in this instance, then I wanted the dream to last as long as possible. For more than two years, I'd played this moment over and over in my head. Hell, only last night, I'd masturbated to the idea of how it'd feel to kiss Trinity, but once I did it for real, there was no going back.

"It should be criminal to be as beautiful as you."

She began to answer, and I stole her words with my mouth as she'd stolen my heart so long ago. She wrapped her arms around my neck, and as we kissed, I realized that every dream I'd ever had was a poor substitute compared to the reality. I splayed my palm against her spine, the other remaining in her hair. Her tits collided with the flat planes of my chest, and a sound reminiscent of a growl reverberated in my throat.

A loud rumble of thunder followed by the crack of lightning brought me to my senses. I let her go, my chest heaving as a second powerful lightning strike lit up the living room, briefly turning night into day. And then darkness fell once more, the only illumination coming from the rapidly dying fire.

Trinity touched her lips and murmured my name. I put several feet between us, her sun-flecked eyes tracking me through every step. It didn't matter that she'd answered my unasked questions about if she found me attractive. That was no longer in doubt. But not even two weeks had passed since Declan had killed himself. And here I was taking advantage of his grieving girlfriend because whatever she said about how far apart they'd grown, and how they hadn't been intimate for months, there must still be a part of her that loved him. And I'd stomped all over his memory.

"I shouldn't have done that."

"Why shouldn't you have? We're both adults. We make our own decisions."

"Yeah," I agreed. "We do. And I just made the wrong one."

Her face twisted, and she wrapped her arms around herself. "I'm sorry you feel that way."

And, without saying another word, she walked out, closing the door silently behind her.

16

Trinity

I didn't get a wink of sleep, and by the time I crawled out of bed the following morning, I felt as if someone had pummeled and punched me while I slept. And in a way, they had. Sebastian's curt dismissal and, worse, his admittance that he'd made a mistake kissing me when, until that moment, those wonderful few seconds had stripped away the months of hurt, had wounded me more than any physical punishment could have done. These last few days, I'd wondered whether there was a spark of attraction between us, and yet now I had the answer I sought, I wished we could go back to how things were.

I'd never been kissed like that in my life. Not that I'd kissed many men. Four to be exact, including Declan, so I had little experience to call upon. But the feelings Sebastian had elicited from a single kiss were more powerful than any of those others. I burned. All night I burned for him. In my heart and my head, and between my legs. I'd tossed and turned, and paced, and on two occasions, I'd opened my door intending to go to him even if I risked the pain of a second rejection. In the end, the only thing that stopped me was out of respect for him. The more I thought about it, the more I grasped his reasoning, although he hadn't vocalized it as such. But an idiot could figure out it had everything to do with Declan, and I understood that more than anyone. I, too, felt the sting of guilt at kissing Declan's brother, but the power of attraction was too strong for me to deny it.

Unfortunately, Sebastian had far better control of his emotions, or maybe the attraction wasn't as strong for him as it was for me. In any case, there was one piece of good news. It'd be easy to avoid him today if, as he'd said last night, he planned to hole up in his study all day working.

I peered out the window at another bright, crisp day. The thunder and lightning that had interrupted our make-out session hadn't materialized into a downpour, or a fresh dumping of snow. Good. That meant I could go for a walk, get some fresh air, and clear my head of all stupid ideas of me and Sebastian. There was no 'us.' There never would be an 'us.' Sure, he kissed like I imagined a Greek God might, and the hard muscle pulled taut over his chest that I'd felt beneath my fingers would linger in my memory for years to come. But thoughts like that were pointless and energy-sapping.

The kitchen showed signs of life, with toast crumbs on the counter, a half-empty pot of coffee, and a knife covered in jam. Sebastian must have been and gone. Part of me was happy that I wouldn't have to face him before I'd figured out what to say. The other part pined for a glimpse of him.

Yeah, I had it bad.

I made a cup of tea, but the idea of food churned my stomach. Maybe later, after a walk had stirred my appetite, I might feel like eating. I downed the tea, stuffed my feet into the sturdy walking boots Sebastian had bought for me, shoved my arms into my coat, and headed outside. The wind bit into my face, and I zipped the coat right to the top, burying my chin inside the fur lining. Spotting Jack over by the annex that he called home, I trudged over, waving a hand in greeting. Boomer barked as I approached, and a frisson of fear made the hairs on the back of my neck stand on end. I was still leery of the giant dog with fangs that I imagined ripping through flesh with ease. As I got closer, he bounded forward, and it took every scrap of courage to keep my feet planted to the ground and not take off in a dead run. On reaching me, he plopped his bum on the snowy ground and gave me his paw.

"He likes you, lassie," Jack said, crunching through the snow toward me. "Go on, now. Shake it or you'll offend him."

I refrained from pointing out to Jack that I wasn't sure dogs took offense at being snubbed and tentatively took Boomer's damp paw.

"There. That wasn't so bad, was it?" He ruffled Boomer's head. "Where are you heading off to?"

"I thought I might go for a walk. Sebastian's hunkered down in his study working today."

Jack frowned. "Funny that, because not a half hour since, he got in his car to drive to the village."

"Oh." I wrinkled my nose. "It's just that last night he said he had to work all day. I guess I assumed that meant on the computer."

"He said something about having to transmit a large file. Down in the village they have one of those, what's it called?" Jack tapped his fingers on the side of his thigh. "A mast. That's it. Sounds more like it belongs on a ship to me, but there you have it."

I grinned. Despite his relative youth, Jack was what I'd call old school. He appeared to enjoy the simpler things in life rather than embrace the technological revolution of the past couple of decades.

"Did he say when he'd be back?"

"No, lassie."

"Oh. Okay, no problem. Well, I think I'll head off."

"Why don't you take Boomer with you? He knows the way home if you get lost."

It was on the tip of my tongue to decline, but then I remembered what Sebastian had said about a bodyguard. It wasn't a bad idea to take the scary beast along with me, just in case. And like Jack said, I wasn't familiar with these parts and could easily get lost.

"He still scares me a bit."

Jack guffawed. "I can tell. Almost turned to stone when he came across to greet you." He gestured by flicking his wrist. "Be gone with you, lassie. He'll not let harm come to you."

He walked away, and when Boomer stayed right by my side, he made the decision for me.

"Come on, boy."

I headed down the path, crossed a wooden stile, and set off over the snow-covered moorland. The ground, frozen solid beneath my feet, suited me fine. I'd much rather frozen than wet and muddy. Boomer trotted along by my side, stopping occasionally to sniff at a stray leaf or a blade of grass sticking up through the snow. The house disappeared into the distance, and suddenly, the idea of bringing Boomer along with me seemed like a very good one.

I'd lived my entire life in London where it was almost impossible to find a spot where you were truly alone. Out here, in the wilderness, with only the birds and an odd rabbit for company, I could be the only person left in the world. And to prove that, I stopped, held my arms out to the side, and screamed. Once I'd emptied my lungs, I sucked in more oxygen and screamed again. Damn, it felt good. All that pent-up sorrow and disappointment and frustration and grief ebbed away, and the weight I'd carried on my back for the last few weeks vanished.

Boomer tilted his head to the side, staring at me with

inquisitive big brown eyes. I laughed and stroked his head, and he leaned into my palm as if craving affection.

"You're just a big old softie, aren't you, boy?"

I walked for another fifteen minutes or so, but when the sky overhead grew dark and heavy with what appeared to be more snow, I spun around and set off the way I'd come from. The return journey was slightly uphill, taking me longer than I thought to make any headway. As the house came into view, big white flakes began to fall, and in seconds, I found myself caught in a blizzard. I upped my pace, my thighs burning from exerting so much effort. I broke into a jog, Boomer loping along beside me, emitting the occasional bark as if to let me know he had my back.

With hardly any visibility, I stumbled through the door and into the warmth of Sebastian's kitchen. Boomer followed me inside, shaking the snow from his fur. Wet blobs went everywhere. I gave him a stern look. In return, he stared up at me with enormous eyes and a lolling tongue.

"Here," I said, filling a bowl with water and placing it at his feet. He immediately lapped at it. "Be good, Boomer. I'm going to take a shower."

I hung my coat on the hook by the door, toed off my boots, and set off upstairs. I did pause halfway up, wondering if Sebastian had returned from town yet and whether I should check his study to find out, but my courage failed me. I still wasn't sure what to say to him, or whether to leave breaking the ice to him. After all, he was the one who'd introduced awkwardness into a difficult situation. He could have rejected me in a far kinder manner than his terse rebuff.

I decided to leave it to him to make overtures and smooth things over. Trudging the rest of the way up the stairs, I turned left, heading for my room when a creak sounded behind me. My heart rate skyrocketed, and I whirled around. No one was there. I crept back along the hallway and peered down the stairs, expecting to see Sebastian hot-footing it in the opposite direction. Nope. Not him. I frowned, then shrugged it off. This was an old house, and everyone knew old houses creaked and groaned all the time.

Dropping my damp clothes on the floor, I switched on the shower, then stepped underneath the hot spray. I let my shoulders droop, my hand braced on the wall, and slowly, the cold gave way to warmth. Sebastian's house might be in the middle of nowhere, but I couldn't fault his heating system. The water here was far hotter than back home in my London flat.

My flat. God, I hated the idea of going back there. I'd never be able to unsee the images of Declan and how terrified he must have been during his final moments as he let the rope take the strain. As soon as it was safe to return, I'd give notice and try to find alternative accommodation. It wouldn't be easy. The London rental scene was the worst kind of dog-eat-dog, with landlords demanding larger and larger rents. I'd be lucky to afford a one-room bedsit on the outskirts of the city, which meant my travel costs to get to work would rise.

I feel used up, exhausted, numb.

Maybe I should try to find a job farther north, where the cost of living wasn't quite so ridiculous. London was the only home I'd ever known, but that didn't mean I shouldn't branch out. A complete change of scenery—as evidenced by these last few days—might be the exact thing I needed to move on with my life and put the last couple of years behind me. I snorted. Two years? Hell, I'd like to put the last twenty years behind me. The day my parents died so unexpectedly was the day everything changed. I'd been completely unprepared for life in the system. Still, I hadn't done that badly. A lot of girls in my position lived their whole lives on state handouts, popping out a few kids before they broke free of their teens, snagging themselves a council house, and never actually living. I'd clawed my way through college, qualified as a counsellor, and contributed to society by helping others. At least I thought so.

Until Declan.

I squeezed my eyes closed and waited for the bite of remorse to recede. Turning off the shower, I grabbed a towel and wrapped it underneath my armpits, swaddling a second one around my dripping wet hair.

I opened the door to the bedroom—and screamed.

17

SEBASTIAN

I veered off the main road that connected the two villages east and west of my house, and began the treacherous drive up the icy lane, the only way in and out to my home by car. Fresh snowfall had made driving even more hazardous, and despite the four-wheel drive SUV, and heavy-duty snow chains—a necessity in this part of Scotland in the depths of winter—a few times I almost lost control, and at one point I only narrowly avoided ending up in a ditch. I chuckled to myself at the thought of calling Jack and asking him for a tow. He'd play on that for years.

But the closer I edged toward home, the more the levity faded, and my mind turned once again to Trinity. For most of the morning, I'd thought of little else, shame at how I'd treated her last night churning in my gut. Yes, she'd kissed me first, but I'd chosen to up the stakes. Hers had been a brush of lips, a testing of the waters. I was the one who'd jumped in with both feet. I'd taken it up a level, hell, several levels, and then I'd surrendered to the guilt that had roared through me, and in the process, I'd hurt the woman I loved. I deserved a slap around the face for the metaphorical one I'd directed at her, yet she'd classily walked away. Her quiet acceptance of my harsh rejection had gnawed at me for the whole fucking night.

Even worse, I'd snuck downstairs this morning, grabbed a quick snack, and slunk out of the house under the bullshit excuse of needing better WiFi. There was nothing wrong with the internet connection at the house. There was, however, a fucking lot wrong with me. In a few months, I'd turn thirty-five years old, and yet I couldn't find the balls to face up to a woman I'd hurt, a woman I happened to love, and tell her that as much as I wanted her, the guilt that I was stealing something that belonged to Declan refused to abate.

Stupid? Probably. But that was the unfortunate truth I had to live with.

Lost in my thoughts, as I approached the house, it took me a few seconds to grasp the scene I'd arrived home to. Blue flashing lights whirred atop the unmistakable yellow and green of an ambulance. My heart stuttered, then raced, adrenaline sending prickles through my body. I rammed my foot on the gas pedal, and the back of the car whipped out, snaking from left to right as the wheels fought for traction. I somehow made it the final hundred yards and slewed to a stop.

I thrust the door open and launched out of the car. My right foot slipped on a patch of ice. I grabbed on to the door to stop myself from falling, found my balance, then sprinted to the ambulance. The back doors were open, but inside was empty. I dashed into the house.

"Trinity!"

I found Jack sitting at my kitchen table, a gray pallor to his normally ruddy cheeks. My stomach dropped to the slate floor beneath my feet.

"What is it? What's happened?"

Jack stood, his hands stretched in front of him in a reassuring motion. "Now, now, laddie. Calm down. She's going to be all right. She's a bit shook up, that's all. She hit her head, so I called the ambulance as a precaution. The paramedics are with her."

"How did she hit her head? What the fuck is going on, Jack? Why didn't you call me?"

"There was an intruder. He cut the phone lines. Boomer saw him off."

"Intruder?" Ice ran through my veins. "Jesus Christ."

I raked both hands through my hair, leaving them there—and then I took off upstairs, bursting into Trinity's room. She turned, saw me, and her eyes filled with tears.

"Fuck, Trinity." I dropped into a squat and clasped her hand. "Are you hurt?"

"She fell and hit her head," one of the paramedics explained, reiterating what Jack had told me.

"How did you fall? Jack said there was an intruder." My stomach twisted at the thought of what might have happened to her.

She gulped and nodded. "Boomer saved me. He bit him. The man kept punching him on the head. Over and over. Is he okay? Is Boomer okay?"

"Boomer's fine." I forced a calmness to my voice while a storm threatened inside. Some *bastard* had entered my home intending to harm a woman. *My fucking woman.* I fisted my free hand. Whoever he was, he'd better hope the cops reached him first. "Don't worry about the dog. Don't worry about anything." I directed my attention to the paramedics. "You're taking her in?"

"Yes, sir. Given that she hit her head, we'd like the doctor to check her out. You can come with us if you'd like."

I nodded curtly. Opening the closet, I pulled out a thick

sweater and a pair of jeans. "Let's get you dressed and then I'll carry you downstairs."

"Oh, Sebastian, no," she complained. "I'm fine. Just a little woozy, that's all."

"No arguments."

She refused my offer of help to dress, and took the clothes into the bathroom. When she reappeared, I helped her put on socks and a pair of sneakers, then I picked her up, ignoring her repeated refusal that she needed the support. Until the hospital checked her out, we didn't know how hard she'd hit her head and I wasn't having her pass out on me and fall down the stairs.

Jack gave her shoulder a quick squeeze as I carried her through the kitchen.

"I'll call you from the hospital, Jack."

Jack didn't bat an eyelid at my brusque tone, nodding in acknowledgement.

I gently set her down in the back of the ambulance and took a seat beside her. I couldn't seem to let go of her hand. She didn't offer any further details, and I didn't question her on what had happened. There was plenty of time for that once the doctors gave her the all clear. For now, all that mattered was Trinity.

An intruder? Cut phone lines. It made no sense. We were in the middle of nowhere, only one road in and out, and as I drove up, I hadn't noticed any tire tracks or footprints in the snow. And why would a stranger want to break into my house and beat up a defenseless woman?

The answer came at me in a rush. The gang. The guns. That was the only explanation I could contrive that didn't sound like we'd entered crazy town.

"Was it them?" I whispered.

She blinked twice, then dropped her chin in a single nod of affirmation.

Fucking hell! I'd promised her, *promised her* she'd be safe.

And if I hadn't fucked off to the village, more interested in avoiding a tough conversation than facing up to what I'd done, she wouldn't have been in the house alone, and none of this would've happened. This was all my fault. All of it.

"Sebastian."

I grazed my knuckles down her arm. "Yeah, honey?"

"I'm glad you're here," she choked out.

I squeezed my eyes closed, an ache setting up home inside my chest, one that I knew would take an eternity to fade. "Take it easy, angel. We'll be at the hospital soon."

It took an hour to reach the Emergency Department of the nearest hospital due to the dangerous driving conditions brought about by the heavy snow and record low temperatures. Inside, there wasn't a spare seat, and the sound of screaming children and overtired parents battered my eardrums. A nurse came over to us, listened to the paramedics' assessment of Trinity's potential injuries, and then directed them to a row of beds separated by dark-green curtains. As I went to follow them, she stopped me.

"I need you to check her in with the receptionist first."

"Can't that wait?" I snapped, and then, realizing it wasn't the nurse's fault that they must follow procedures, I shot her a quick smile. "Sorry. I'm worried about her, that's all."

"Girlfriend?"

It crossed my mind that if I said no, they might not allow me to see her, and so I nodded.

"We'll take good care of her. Come and find me once you're done."

I lined up behind four other people, also waiting for the overworked receptionist to get to them. It took fifteen minutes before my turn arrived. I gave her as much information as I could, but when it came to allergies to drugs, or previous medical history, I didn't have a clue.

I walked in the direction I'd seen the paramedics take Trinity, but the nurse who'd first assessed her was nowhere around. I poked my head inside a couple of the cubicles, apologizing to the occupants when neither of them turned out to be Trinity. I was about to look inside the third when I spotted the nurse.

"Where is she?"

She frowned, as if she didn't know what I was talking about, and then she acknowledged me.

"Ah yes, the young lady you came in with. We've sent her for a CT scan, just to be sure there's no fracture from when she fell. You can wait in the family room until she returns."

She set off at a clip down a corridor, turned left at the end, then opened a door where a couple were sitting close together, their heads bowed, and the young woman was quietly sobbing.

"How long will she be?"

Her forehead puckered. "Your guess is as good as mine. As you can see, we're run off our feet tonight. It's the weather." She smiled at my dismayed expression. "Hopefully not too long. There's a vending machine back in reception if you'd like a drink."

"Thanks."

I took a seat on the opposite side of the room from the couple, affording them at least some privacy, and put in a call to Jack. I updated him on Trinity's condition, and he told me a police officer had called by.

"He wanted to talk to you both, but I said you were at the hospital. You'd think they'd know." He harrumphed. "Left hand doesn't know what the bloody right hand is doing. He asked to take a look around the house, but I told him he'd have to talk to you about that. Left you a number to call."

"Okay." I reached behind me and squeezed the tight muscles at the back of my neck. "Thanks, Jack. I'll call you when we're on our way home. Lock up and don't answer the door to anyone."

Jack guffawed. "Good luck to 'em if they wanna come at me, laddie. I got Boomer with me."

Thank God for that dog. When I'd joked with Trinity on Friday about him acting as her bodyguard, I never thought he'd actually get called into action.

"Give him an extra bone from me."

I hung up and stared out the grubby window. The snow had stopped falling, but the sky overhead was still heavy, the clouds grey and ominous. An hour later, the same nurse returned. I scrambled to my feet before she'd even closed the door.

"How is she?"

"She's fine. We're going to keep her in overnight for observation, but she should be able to go home tomorrow morning. She has a mild concussion, so you'll need to monitor her for a few days. We'll give you a list of things to look out for."

"Can I see her?"

"Of course. Follow me."

She led me to a small ward with only four beds. If Trinity were in any longer than a night, I'd arrange a private room, but the nurses here had more than enough to do without me making a fuss. I pulled up a chair. At the sound the legs made on the tiled floor, Trinity turned toward me, and once again, her eyes filled with tears.

"Hey now." I clasped her tiny hand in mine. "You're safe."

"Stay with me," she pleaded.

I kissed her forehead. "I'm not going anywhere."

She sighed and closed her eyes. As much as I craved answers, they'd have to wait. After a good night's sleep, she'd feel up to telling me as much as she recalled about what had happened.

I'd underestimated this gang, assuming I could protect Trinity by getting her out of London while the private investigator found those guns, or the situation forced us to switch to

Plan B and involve the police. Yet they'd easily tracked us up here. As painful as it was, I had to admit that I wasn't able to offer her the protection she needed.

But I knew a man who could.

18

SEBASTIAN

"Sebastian."

Roused from sleep, I willed my eyes to open, even as they fought against me. My back felt trampled on, and as I moved my neck, it violently protested. Groaning, I sat up straight and massaged it, trying to get the kinks out.

"You look terrible."

I blinked to clear my vision, rubbing my eyes, and struggling to come to full consciousness. I remembered watching the clock tick past four a.m., and it now read six-thirty, which explained why I was so damned tired.

"You should have gone home. That chair is no place for a man of your size."

"Never mind me." I curled my fingers around hers. "How are you feeling?"

"Fine." A smile touched her lips. "A bit of a fraud, if you must know."

I ground my teeth, still furious with myself that I'd left her, and all because I was too chicken-shit to stick around and face up to our situation. If I had stayed home, she wouldn't be here.

"Do you feel up to telling me what happened?"

Her eyes flickered to the other patients in the small ward. They all looked to still be sleeping, although it was hard to tell. I stood and closed the privacy curtains around her bed.

"We can wait, if you'd like."

"No, it's fine." She ran her tongue over her lips. "Can you pour me a glass of water?"

"Sure." I did as she asked.

She only took a few sips, then flopped back against the stack of pillows. I returned the glass to the nightstand and retook my seat.

"I went for a walk with Boomer." She kept her voice low to avoid being overheard. "I was out for a couple of hours, I guess. After we got back, I left him in the kitchen with a bowl of water and went upstairs to shower. When I walked back into the bedroom, a man was waiting for me."

She closed her eyes, probably reliving the moment, the shock, the fear of finding herself alone in the house with an intruder.

"Same guy that accosted you in London?"

"Yes. The one with the knife. This time, he had a gun."

"Jesus." A tremor shot up my spine at what might have happened to her. What I might've come home to. *I feel sick.*

"He told me I couldn't run and I couldn't hide. That they'd always find me. Then he demanded again to know where the guns were. I told him I didn't know, but that we had someone searching for them and we needed more time. He called me a liar, then backhanded me. I fell and hit my head on the window ledge."

A trickle of blood ran down my hand and only then did I realize I'd dug my nails so deeply into my palm, I'd made it bleed.

He fucking hit her. I'll kill him.

I locked on the faint bruise on her face, and a fresh deluge of burning rage flooded my veins. This was all my fault. I'd opened the door, and that bastard had walked right in.

My eyes lowered to the floor. "I'm so sorry. If I hadn't left you…"

"No," she said firmly. "This isn't on you. It's on them. It's on Declan. You and I, we're innocents in all this. I won't have you blaming yourself."

"I didn't have to go to the village yesterday," I admitted, even as it pained me to do so. "I was avoiding you. After what happened the other night."

She twisted her lips to the side. "Yeah, I figured."

"So you see, this *is* on me. If I'd been there, then none of this would have happened."

"Stop." Her hand came up. "I told you in London that you couldn't watch over me twenty-four-seven. What happened today proves that." Her eyebrows drew together, and she fisted the covers with her free hand. "They'll come for me again, Sebastian. I know it."

I wished I could disagree with her, but I couldn't—because she was dead on. "I know. That's why I've changed our plans."

"You're calling the police?"

"Not yet, although I'll take that under advisement when we go to see Loris. One thing I won't do is put your life in danger." *Any more than I already have.*

She frowned. "Who's Loris?"

"A friend. Well, an acquaintance really. He runs a security firm called Intrepid that offers all kinds of protection services from close personal protection to crowd management and everything in between. He's got all kinds of celebrities, politicians, and even royalty on his books. I've called him already, and he's expecting us at his headquarters later today. Once we've spoken with him, if he advises bringing the police into it, then I will."

"Today?"

"Yes. As soon as you've given your statement to the police about what happened—and we need to decide on what you're going to say—we're flying back to London."

She groaned. "In the helicopter?"

Despite the seriousness of the situation, her dismay brought a smile to my lips.

"It'll be better the second time around."

"You think?"

I chuckled. "What's that English phrase? Time to gird your loins. Did I get that right?"

She grinned. "You did. And gird them I shall—through gritted teeth."

I picked up her hand and kissed her knuckles, savoring the intimacy of the moment and lingering longer than I should have.

"Trinity, once we're back in London, we need to t—"

The curtains swished open, and a nurse bustled in. "Good morning, sweetheart. How are you feeling this morning?"

I dropped her hand, cursing the untimely interruption, and forced a smile at the nurse.

"Much better, thank you," Trinity murmured.

"Your man here never left your side all night. You've got a good one there. I'd hang on to him if I were you."

Trinity looked over at me with a wry twist of her lips. "We're just friends. But you're right, he's a good person."

Friends? Fuck being friends. I had enough of those. What I didn't have was... her.

I turned away, cramming down disappointment into the pit of my stomach. After rejecting her the way I had the other night, I deserved the public rebuke, but a conversation was on the horizon, one I refused to shy away from any longer. Once we'd met with Loris and figured out the next steps, I'd find the right moment, and this time, I'd ensure that no one interrupted us.

The nurse picked up Trinity's wrist and took her pulse, then wrapped a blood pressure cuff around her upper arm. She scribbled the results on a clipboard hanging at the end of her bed. "Any headaches? Blurred vision? Nausea."

"No."

She nodded, seemingly satisfied with Trinity's responses. "The doctor will be here in the next hour or so for his rounds. Providing he's happy, you should be able to go home this morning."

∼

The nurse lied about the hour. It was closer to two before the doctor came to examine Trinity, and that was after several not-so-subtle nudges from me every time I spotted a member of staff passing by the ward. He examined her, then gave her the all clear and, after signing a few release forms, we caught a cab back to my house. There'd been a partial thaw overnight, and the roads were more slushy than icy, meaning it only took forty minutes to arrive home. I'd barely gotten her out of the cab when Boomer bounded over, closely followed by Jack. In complete contrast to the first time she met the dog on Friday, Trinity crouched and gave him the kind of hug that actually made me jealous. Me? Jealous of a damned dog. What a joke.

"Is he okay?" Trinity asked Jack as she ruffled Boomer's thick fur. "The intruder hit him pretty hard when Boomer wouldn't let him go."

"He's fine, lassie." Jack smiled. "He's got a tough head just like me."

"You're a hero, Boomer," she murmured, giving him a final squeeze.

She straightened, and I slipped my arm around her waist. "Let's get you inside." I cocked my head at Jack, indicating that he should follow. The three of us, and Boomer, went into the house. Jack had already lit a fire in the kitchen and in the living room, where I took Trinity under the pretext of it being more comfortable. I wanted a word with Jack without her overhearing.

"I'll go make some tea."

She nodded, yawning. "Sounds good."

I returned to the kitchen and closed the door. "Have the police been back?"

Jack shook his head and handed me a card. "That's the copper who wants you to call."

I set it on the table, then sat down. Jack followed suit. My back protested from sleeping at an awkward angle. *Christ, I'm exhausted.* "I'll call him in a minute. We're leaving for London this afternoon, so if he can't get here before then, he'll have to take her statement over the phone."

Jack narrowed his eyes and leaned forward as if to get a better read on my expression. "This wasn't a random attack, eh?"

"No." I palmed the back of my neck as I apprised him of the barest details. "I need you to do something for me after we leave."

"And what's that, laddie?"

"Take off for a few days. A week tops. On my dime, of course."

Jack shook his head. "Some eejit isn't gonna chase me from my home."

"He's hardly an idiot, Jack. He had a gun, and he found us in a matter of days. Whoever this gang is, they're connected. I'm already flaying myself over what happened to Trinity. Don't add yourself to that list. Please, for me."

He harrumphed. "Fine. If it makes you feel better, I'll give you a week."

I stood and clapped him on the shoulder. "Good man." Drawing the police officer's business card toward me, I scanned it. "I'd better call Officer McFadden."

I saw Jack out, then flipped the card over in my hand. Before I called him, I had something to do. Dashing upstairs, I kneeled beside Trinity's bed and peered underneath. Sure enough, there was the gun. I returned to the kitchen, grabbed a wooden spoon, a pair of gloves, and a plastic bag. I used the spoon to pull the gun toward me and, slipping a gloved finger underneath the trigger, I dropped it into the bag and sealed it. Loris might find it useful. He had access to all kinds of criminal records. No idea how, but it didn't matter. If anyone had the skills and the contacts to keep Trinity safe and pour additional resources into finding the gang and the guns, it was Loris Winslow. I should have thought of him first.

I stuffed the bag containing the gun underneath the helicopter seat, then made the call. The police officer arrived within the hour. Trinity gave her statement, sticking to the story we'd agreed on. She arrived home from her walk to find an intruder in the house. He hit her, then ran. I chimed in to confirm that nothing was missing, or at least as far as I was aware, and from the lack of follow-up questions from the cop, I believed we'd convinced him it was nothing more than an opportunist. A hiker out for a walk who decided to chance his luck and panicked when Trinity came home and disturbed him. I promised to call if anything else came to mind, and he left after fifteen minutes.

Trinity and I watched him get into his car and drive away.

"Well then," she murmured. "London it is."

19

TRINITY

I did it. I survived.

On wobbly legs, I climbed out of the death trap masquerading as a means of transportation and into the car Sebastian had waiting for us, and as I did, I promised myself that I'd taken my second—and last—helicopter ride.

"You're not as green as you were when we hit that bit of turbulence." Sebastian's lips quirked in that way he had that reeked of teasing—at my expense.

"A bit of turbulence?" I arched an eyebrow. "Understatement of the year."

He chuckled, and the tension across my shoulders lifted a little. Since we'd kissed, the atmosphere between us had been strained, but it looked as if things had gone back to the way they were before, and I, for one, was relieved, even if the sting of his rejection still hurt.

As the car moved off, I twisted in my seat. "Tell me about this man, Loris. How do you know him?"

"I don't know him well, but I guess you could say we're acquaintances. I first met him around eighteen months ago at an event hosted by the Mayor of London. He's part of the British aristocracy, but you'd never know it if it wasn't public record. His official title is the Seventeenth Earl of Montford, and he's one of the richest men in Europe, but he didn't let that stop him joining the Royal Marines when he was eighteen which, he once told me, his late father was apoplectic about. He served with them for almost a decade but left when his sister was murdered three years ago."

"Oh God. How awful for him."

Sebastian nodded. "That was why he started his security firm, Intrepid. His sister, Sophia, was a classical music star. One night, after she sang at the Royal Albert Hall, a so-called fan broke into her hotel room. He raped and strangled her."

"Oh God. Yes. I remember now. It was all over the papers."

"Yeah, it was big news at the time. Loris carried out his own investigation into what happened and discovered that her security had really dropped the ball which Loris believed led directly to her death. He was determined no one else would suffer like he and his family had at the hands of mediocre protection services. He left the Royal Marines on compassionate grounds, and Intrepid was born. He hires only the best of the best. Former Marines, Navy SEALs, SAS, Mossad operatives. You get the picture."

"That's why you called him."

"Yeah. I trust him to give us the right advice. He'll know the best way to deal with this and, like I said to you in the hospital, if he tells me to get the police involved, then that's what I'll do. Mom will have to deal with it."

"I hope it doesn't come to that," I murmured. Serena deserved to mourn her son without knowing the awfulness surrounding his death. She shouldn't have to live the rest of her life aware of the man he'd become, rather than the son she thought him to be.

"We'll see," Sebastian replied noncommittally.

We left the city landscape behind and headed south to the rolling countryside of Surrey. After we'd traveled for almost an hour, the driver turned off the main road and steered the car up a narrow lane, with tall hedges on either side. He eventually stopped outside a set of imposing gates. Sebastian rolled down the window and announced our arrival into an intercom mounted on a wall, and the gates soundlessly swung inward. On either side of the wide tarmac driveway were pristine lawned gardens that stretched as far as the eye could see. And... wait... was that a golf course on the brow of the hill?

"Where are we?" I asked.

"Montford Hall. This is Loris's family estate, although these days he uses it as Intrepid's headquarters."

"You've been here before?"

"No. First timer, like you. He's a very private man and is rarely seen in public these days. He wasn't exactly a regular on the aristocratic circuit before Sophia's death. Too busy serving in the Royal Marines, but since that awful tragedy, and the immense success of Intrepid, he occupies his time running the company and the estate."

"He sounds like Bruce Wayne," I said, chuckling. "Does he have a Batmobile and an underground cave?"

Sebastian threw back his head and laughed. "You'll have to ask him."

I widened my eyes. "I wouldn't dream of it. And don't you say anything either. That was a joke between you and me."

His eyes twinkled, and he winked. My stomach flipped over, as if we'd driven too fast down a steep dip in the road. God, I wanted him. I'd started to wonder if what I'd felt for Declan had ever been real. I'd fancied him, at least at the beginning of our relationship, but this heat that seemed to consume me whenever Sebastian looked at me the way he was right now was a whole new experience. The futility of my obsession sat like a concrete block on my chest. He'd made his feelings very clear, and hoping for a different outcome was a pointless waste of energy. Besides, these weren't normal circumstances, and what I thought I felt for Sebastian could end up little more than fake emotions brought about by the situation I found myself in. The last couple of weeks had taken their toll on us both, and I didn't know what to believe anymore. The heart lied sometimes, and with the shadow of death hanging over me, now wasn't the time to make decisions—or worse, make a fool of myself.

Five minutes after we drove through the gates, an imposing brick house came into view. Except house wasn't the right description, and even mansion didn't come close. Montford Hall was *enormous*. Slack jawed, I stared out the window as the car drew to a halt.

"Wow."

Sebastian snickered. "And you thought I was rich."

He got out and came around my side of the car to open my door. Good thing, too, because I was still too dumbfounded to even unclip my seat belt. By the time I persuaded my legs to work, a man in his late twenties or maybe early thirties had appeared and was making his way over to us. Loris Winslow, at least I presumed this was him, was nothing like I'd expected. Taller than Sebastian by several inches, his shoulders were broad, his chest profoundly muscled. His hair was almost black, and his angular jaw was covered in a close-cut beard. I had to drag my gaze away from his perfect face in case he caught me gawking. He reminded me of a flawless statue, but as gorgeous as he was, he lacked Sebastian's warmth. In fact, he intimidated the hell out of me.

"Sebastian." His voice boomed, and he thrust out his hand for Sebastian to shake. "It's good to see you."

"And you, Loris."

He turned his startling blue gaze on me, and I took a step back. He was... a lot to take in. I couldn't think of another way to describe him. I bet when he'd served in the Royal Marines, he'd scared the shit out of the enemy with a single icy stare.

"You must be Trinity. Why don't you both come inside and we can talk?"

He pivoted and strode away without waiting to see whether we even followed. Not that we wouldn't, but even so.

"He's... interesting," I whispered. "Is he really an earl?"

I said interesting, but I meant terrifying. Thank God he was on our side. I wouldn't want to make an enemy of him.

Sebastian released a low chuckle. "Yes, he really is an earl."

The entranceway of Montford Hall was exactly what I imagined a house as old as this would look like. All mahogany wood paneling, dark, embossed wallpaper the color of seaweed, and low-hanging chandeliers that emitted very little light. I didn't know what made me do it, but I reached for Sebastian's hand. I wouldn't swear to it, but he might've stiffened. Then he wrapped strong fingers around mine and squeezed.

"Definitely Bruce Wayne vibes," he murmured, his lips quirked in a faint smile.

I snorted a laugh, horrified when Loris Winslow glanced over his shoulder and frowned.

"Right this way," he said in a distinct cut-crystal English accent favored by the British aristocracy.

He motioned us inside a room decorated in a similar style. Bookshelves covered every inch of wall space, each one filled to the brim with books—no doubt mostly first editions—and a Chesterfield sofa and chair completed the austere vibe. A fire burned in the grate, adding much needed warmth, but despite that, I shivered.

Loris took the chair, leaving the sofa free for me and Sebastian. Crossing his legs, he knitted his fingers together and laid them in his lap.

"Tell me how I can help."

I left Sebastian to do the talking, only chipping in when asked to contribute directly. I noticed Loris didn't take any notes, but his insightful questions showed that he'd taken it all in. Maybe his training in the military meant he didn't need to write anything down. I did get a shock when Sebastian handed over the gun. I'd forgotten all about it. Loris peered at the weapon through the plastic bag, then set it on the table.

"I'll get my forensic team on this. If there're prints, they'll find them. Has the private investigator uncovered where the weapons are yet?" Loris asked when Sebastian finished.

"Not so far. He's sent in a couple of reports with updates. Nothing concrete. I said I'd call him today, but with everything that's happened during the last twenty-four hours, I haven't had a chance."

Loris pressed his palms together, then steepled his fingers underneath his chin. He expelled a deep breath through his nose. "Okay, here's the plan. I want to move you to one of my safe houses. This gang tracked you to Scotland with no trouble, which means they're not to be taken lightly, and therefore, going home isn't a good idea. I'll put two of my guys with you for the duration while we flush them out. Leave me the investigator's number and I'll engage."

"Okay." Sebastian removed a business card from his wallet and handed it to Loris. "Here are his details."

"Thanks." He gave it a cursory glance then set it on the arm of the chair. "I need your mobile phones."

My eyebrows shot up. "Why?"

Loris gave me those piercing eyes again, and I cursed that I'd spoken up. Drawing this man's attention toward me wasn't something I was awfully keen to do.

"I want to check them for tracker software. And I need to

check your clothes, too. Everything you brought back from Scotland."

"Tracker software?" My throat constricted at the idea of such a thing. Of those men watching us, waiting for an opportunity to pounce. "You're saying they're tracking us?"

"No. I'm saying I leave nothing to chance. Somehow they found you, and pretty fast. I'm eliminating possibilities, that's all."

Sebastian handed over his phone without hesitation. I kept mine in my handbag. This man was a stranger to me, and my phone contained personal stuff as well as the only photograph I had of my parents and me. I'd had the scruffy photograph restored and then loaded onto my mobile phone. To this day, I still didn't know what had happened to my parents' possessions. One of the carers at the children's home thought they might have been put in storage, but I'd never managed to locate them. Hence how precious this one picture was to me.

"I'm not comfortable with this."

"It's okay, Trinity," Sebastian said. "Whatever is on there will be in the cloud, so if Loris fucks up, it's all good." He laughed, and for the first time since we'd arrived, Loris's lips twitched.

"I don't fuck up," he clipped.

"It isn't backed up," I admitted, my voice small and embarrassed. I'd meant to. Countless times. But unlike most people my age, technology and I weren't the best of bedfellows. "Everything is on my phone." I held up my hands in surrender. "I know, I know. It's dumb."

Loris smiled, a proper one, and it changed his entire face, making him look almost human.

"I'll back it up before I do anything. I give you my word that I won't lose a single thing. And I'll set up storage for you so you're fully protected in the future."

His reassurances still felt like cold comfort and, with some reluctance, I reached into my handbag and retrieved my phone. "I guess it's okay. But please, be careful."

Loris disappeared with our phones, leaving us behind. Once I made sure he was out of earshot, I directed my attention to Sebastian, feeling the need to explain myself. "It's the picture of my parents I'm worried about losing. It's the only one I have of them. I don't care about anything else on there."

Sebastian's gaze rested on my face, and for a beat, I struggled to breathe.

"What happened to all their things?"

"I don't know. Sold, sent to landfill." I shrugged, the nonchalant action belying the ache in my chest. "All I remember having with me at the first home they sent me to was a small suitcase with some of my clothes and that one photograph."

The softness in Sebastian's eyes made me want to burst into tears. And when he held out his arms, I couldn't resist, even though I should. I nestled against his warmth and clung to him.

"You're one hell of a woman, Trinity Lane. Most would've crumbled by now, yet you just keep on going. But it's okay to accept help from others. It's okay to lean on someone else for a while. How would you feel about me putting the feelers out and seeing if we can't find out what happened to all your mom and dad's personal items? I have a couple of guys in mind who relish this kind of thing. You never know. I can't make any promises, but it's worth a try. They might strike gold."

My breath caught, and I swallowed past a lump in my throat. "Would you?"

"Of course. Jot down everything you can remember. Your address, the homes you stayed at. Anything like that."

The tightness in my chest increased. Here was a good man, a kind man, and because of me—or rather because of Declan— his whole life had been turned upside down.

"I'm so sorry I dragged you into all this. Your house in Scotland broken into because of me, and now you can't even go back to your home in London."

"Shh."

He smoothed a hand over my hair and kissed the top of my head, and a dash of hope lit me up inside.

"And for the last time, you didn't drag me into anything. Declan did."

"All the same, I—"

"Here we are. Oh, sorry to interrupt."

I scrambled to sit upright as Loris returned with our phones, my face flushing with heat. Not that I had any reason for embarrassment, but that didn't stop a hot blush from spreading down to my neck.

"Your phones were clean, so that's not how they found you. And I backed everything up for you, Trinity. You'll find an email with all the details of where your data is stored and how to access it in your inbox."

My eyebrows shot up. "How did you get my email address?"

Loris's lips curved up on one side. "I run a security firm. It isn't that hard."

A shudder ran through me. "Nothing's really private, is it?"

"Not if you know what you're doing." He patted my shoulder. "Don't worry. You're in safe hands."

I tried to smile but struggled to sustain it. *God, I'm exhausted.*

"Both of you stand up for me."

He held out a wand, kind of like those used at airports. It crackled as he scanned our entire bodies, from head to foot.

"Nothing. Wait here. I'll go check your luggage."

He reappeared after a few minutes and shook his head. "Is there any other way they might have found you? Did you tell anyone where you were going?"

"No," Sebastian said. "I told no one."

"Neither did I," I offered.

"Hmm." He rubbed his fingers over his lips.

"My coat." I gripped Sebastian's arm. "I just remembered I left my coat hanging up in the kitchen. I've been wearing the one you bought me since we arrived. Could that be it? It's the same coat I wore when those men cornered me in that alleyway."

Sebastian stiffened underneath my fingers, and his lips flattened.

"I'll have it couriered down immediately," he said.

"Have it sent here," Loris said.

"Will do."

A buzzer sounded, and Loris tapped his watch, then rubbed his hands together. "Okay, folks, time to go."

20

Sebastian

"Is this room okay for you?"

I put Trinity's bag down beside the king-sized bed and shot her a smile. She'd been quiet ever since we left Montford Hall, and I'd begun to worry. She'd been through a ton of shit in the last three weeks. Even the strongest had a limit. I couldn't shake the feeling that she was approaching hers.

She wandered over to the window and peered out onto the street below. I'd imagined a safe house to be in the middle of nowhere, but this one wasn't far from my place in Holland Park.

"How long do you think we'll have to stay here?"

"Until the guns are located, or the threats neutralized, I guess."

"Hmm." She swiveled around and sat on the window ledge. "You can go home if you want. It's me they're after."

My eyebrows shot north. "Is that what you want?"

She covered her mouth and nose with her hands, then scrubbed her cheeks as if she was trying to warm them. "I know you think you're responsible for me because of Declan, but I'm safe here. Loris's men will ensure nothing happens to me. You've done your duty. You're off the hook."

I narrowed my eyes and pursed my lips. "Done my duty? What the hell is that supposed to mean?"

Trinity averted her gaze, correctly reading the annoyance written all over my face.

"I just meant... oh, I don't know. You have a life, Sebastian. A business to run, responsibilities, people relying on you for their jobs. You don't have time to babysit me, and you shouldn't have to."

Three strides brought me directly in front of her. I squatted and rested my hands on her knees. "Has it occurred to you that I'm here because there's nowhere else I'd rather be?"

She released a heavy sigh, and her shoulders dropped with the effort. "I don't want you to feel obligated, that's all."

"I don't."

The heat from her legs warmed my palms, and my fingers ached to explore. How easy it would be to slide my hands up her thighs. Would she resist or assent? I tuned my ears in to her breathing, to the intensity in her eyes as she watched my fingers curl, squeezing her tighter. She fidgeted, breaking the spell. I silently cursed another bout of bad timing on my part and released her, pushing upright.

"Why don't you unpack? We can grab a bite to eat and then turn in for the night. It'll all seem better in the morning."

"Sounds good."

I walked away, then glanced over my shoulder. There was so much I wanted to say to her, but it never felt like the right time. Fate seemed determined to put blocks in the way—or maybe I lacked the balls to dive in and take what should have always been mine—but every time I teetered on the edge of telling her how I really felt, I bottled it.

"I'll see you downstairs."

I left her alone, dropped my bag in the room next door, and went in search of the bodyguards, Sully and Crew, who'd greeted us on arrival. I'd never deemed a bodyguard necessary, although Ryker, another of the ROGUES board members, had used them on occasion, mainly when traveling to far-flung corners of the world. I preferred my privacy.

The smell of freshly brewed coffee drew me to the kitchen, and that was where I found our security detail, sitting at the small pine table in the center of the room. They smiled in greeting.

"Mr. Devereaux, do you need anything, sir?"

"Sebastian, please." I poured myself a cup of coffee and joined them. "This must be strange, huh?"

"Not for us," Crew said. "For you, yes, I can imagine this doesn't happen every day."

"I'm not sure what to do."

Sully took a huge bite out of a cookie, brushing the crumbs off his T-shirt. "Go about your business as you normally would. If you need to leave the safe house for any reason, then one of us will accompany you, and the other will remain behind with Miss Lane, although try to keep any sorties to a minimum. Apart from that, do what you'd normally do at," he checked his watch, "six-thirty on a Tuesday night."

Six-thirty. Jesus, is that all it is?

Crew whacked Sully on the arm. "Let's leave the man to it." He swigged the rest of his coffee and put the mug into the dishwasher. "If you need us, holler."

I poked my head in the fully stocked fridge and withdrew some ham and cheese. I'd cook a proper meal tomorrow, but a sandwich would do for now. Despite the early hour, all I wanted was food and sleep. The disturbed night at the hospital must have caught up with me.

Trinity joined me a few minutes later, still looking tired but brighter. It took everything I had not to dash over to her and wrap her in my arms, kiss the ever-loving shit out of her, and take her to bed. Yet despite my yearning for her, an invisible force stopped me from acting on a longing so fierce, it stole the breath right from my lungs, leaving me lightheaded and dizzy.

"I don't suppose there's a cup of tea going, is there?" She pulled out a chair and flopped into it.

"Absolutely." I set down the two plates of sandwiches, made her tea, and refilled my coffee cup.

"We're alone?" she asked.

"Yeah." I bit into my sandwich. "They were here when I came downstairs. We're to holler if we need them."

She swiped a hand over her face. "God, this is weird."

"I know." I grinned in an attempt to take the edge off. "They told me to just do what I normally do."

"And what is that?"

"You don't want to hear about my boring life," I countered.

"I do. Go on, tell me," she added when my expression must've shown surprise at her interest. "I really want to know. What does A Day in the Life of Sebastian Devereaux look like under normal circumstances?"

"I warn you, it's a surefire way of sending you to sleep."

"Stop teasing." She swatted my arm. "Please. It'll take my mind off everything."

"Okay. You asked for it." I lifted the coffee to my lips and sipped. "I usually get up around six. Workout for an hour in my gym. Shower, dress, eat, then head into the office." I chuckled. "I told you it was boring."

Trinity leaned her elbow on the kitchen table and propped up her chin with her hand. "I'm not bored. Go on. What happens at the office?"

"Rounds of meetings, emails, contract negotiations, business planning and strategy calls with the other ROGUES board members."

"They're your friends, correct? I remember Declan saying something about how you met them at college."

"Yeah."

"It must be nice to work with friends."

She sounded so melancholy, and I recalled her telling me she hadn't had any friends growing up. How lonely she must have been. It... it killed me to think of it.

"It is." I polished off the rest of the sandwich.

"And what about after work, or at the weekends? What do you do to relax?"

Think about you.

A flush of heat crept up my neck at the uninvited thought And she noticed.

"You're blushing. What were you thinking of, right then?"

"Nothing," I mumbled, hiding my embarrassment under a flurry of plate and cup gathering. I stacked them in the dishwasher.

"I'm sorry."

I closed the dishwasher door and faced her. "For what?"

"You were thinking of her, weren't you? The girl who got away."

Oh, fuck.

"No... I-I. Look, Trinity, there's something you should kn—"

Crash!

We both started at the loud noise.

"What the hell was that?" she asked, the color draining from her face.

"Stay here," I ordered.

"No. I'm coming with you."

We only got as far as the doorway when Crew and Sully appeared, guns drawn.

"Get back," Sully barked, gesturing with his arm.

Trinity and I stepped back into the kitchen, and he slammed the door, leaving us inside.

"What's happening?" Trinity asked, panicked. "Have they found us?"

"I don't know."

I grabbed a knife from the block on the countertop and stood between the door and her. If anyone other than Crew or Sully came through that door intending to hurt Trinity, they'd have to get through me first. I strained my ears, listening for sounds of a scuffle or, God forbid, gunfire, except the only thing I heard was the sound of my accelerated breathing as adrenaline coursed through my body.

The door opened, and I brandished the knife.

"Fuck, Crew. What's going on?" I dropped my arm, the knife dangling by my side.

Crew stepped forward, removed it from my grip, and slotted it into the knife block.

"A shelf with some books had fallen off the wall in one of the spare bedrooms. Happened to me, once, in the middle of the night. Nearly gave me a heart attack. I'll fix it in the morning." He grinned. "Then again, with my DIY skills, maybe I'll leave it to someone else." He dipped his chin. "I'll say goodnight. See you both in the morning."

Trinity reached out a trembling hand, gripped the edge of the table, and collapsed into a chair. "God, I thought... I thought..."

I pulled out the chair next to hers and rubbed her shoulder, then massaged the tight muscles. "You're safe. I promise."

She pursed her lips and blew out a slow breath. "I don't think my heart can take much more."

A deepening ache spread through my chest. *Neither can mine.* I'd almost told her how I felt again and been thwarted. Again.

"I suggest we turn in. Come on."

I got to my feet and, together, we trudged upstairs. I waited until she closed her bedroom door, then entered my own room.

I showered and climbed under the covers. The unfamiliar surroundings, too-firm mattress, and the threat of imminent danger kept me from falling asleep. I was about to give up on the idea of sleep and work instead when a tapping came at my door.

"Yeah?"

Trinity poked her head inside my bedroom. I sat up and switched on the bedside lamp.

"Hey, what's wrong?"

"Drugs, guns, bodyguards, safe houses, shelves falling off the wall. My nerves are hanging by a thread." Her chin wobbled, and she wrung her hands. "Can I stay with you? I don't want to be by myself. Not tonight. I'll sleep on the floor."

For my own sanity, I should have told her no. Instead, I chose the insane route. I peeled back the covers and patted the space beside me. "Get in before you catch cold."

She scampered over and climbed into bed. *My bed.* Surely she'd hear my heart pounding, the way my voice had dropped an octave, how my skin flushed as she lay down beside me, her luminous golden eyes boring into mine.

I cleared my throat, then turned over and switched off the lamp, throwing us into darkness. For the sake of my sanity, I shuffled to the edge of the mattress.

"Sebastian?"

"Yeah?" My voice scratched, a tell of desire, of how much being this close to her and yet not able to touch her affected me.

"Goodnight," she whispered.

"Night."

I lay there, tortured, aching. My dick throbbed, my balls begged for release, and my heart pounded at twice its normal speed. The mattress dipped and creaked, and... oh fuck... she pressed herself into my back. Her breasts flattened against me, her breathing wafting over my skin, and a wave of goose bumps appeared along my arms.

Sweet Jesus fucking Christ. I'm a goner.

I held myself stiff, barely breathing, unmoving. Already on the edge of the bed, I had nowhere to go. My throat narrowed, and I forced a swallow. I counted another five excruciating minutes until her breathing evened out. I'd give it another five and then try to shift her onto her side of the bed without waking her.

"Trinity?" I softly questioned when the allotted time had passed. She didn't reply. Carefully, I wriggled onto my other side, coming face to face with her. Stealing a rare, uninterrupted moment, I studied her face in the semi-darkness. The curve of her mouth, the cut of her cheekbones, the slope of her neck. I loved her so deeply, it physically hurt.

"It haunts me that you met him first. But you did, and there's nothing either of us can do about that." I sighed heavily and pressed a kiss to her hair. "Sweet dreams, beautiful."

21

Trinity

Rain battered the windowpanes, the downpour relentless. The noise woke me, and I slowly came to, blinking two or three times. My lids felt heavy, almost as if someone had sewn tiny lead weights into my eyelashes while I slept.

Heat surrounded me, legs tangled with mine, a large hand rested against my stomach, underneath my camisole top, and the unmistakable feeling of a hard, enormous erection pressed into my backside.

The events of last night came rushing back, and I moved my head, an inch at a time, glancing over my shoulder.

Sebastian.

He appeared to be asleep. Maybe I could sneak out, return to my room, and convince him it'd all been a dream. Except I couldn't figure out how to work myself free without waking him, considering he was wrapped around me like an out-of-control vine.

I shifted and wriggled.

He moved his hand up and cupped my breast.

Oh God.

In that split second, I stopped breathing. Every nerve ending fired up simultaneously, sending electrical pulses racing through my body. My clit throbbed, and my nipples hardened.

"Sebastian?" I whispered.

He didn't reply.

I glanced behind me for a second time. His eyes were still closed, his dark lashes almost touching the swell of his cheeks.

"Are you awake?"

He responded by kneading my breast, and he pressed his groin closer to me. The ridge of his erection nestled between the crease of my arse. I lay there, unsure what to do. If his subconscious was in charge, then it seemed wrong of me to allow him to continue caressing me, potentially thinking I was someone else. The woman he'd loved and lost, maybe. But what if he was awake, knowingly touching me? What then? Nothing had changed—and yet everything had.

I want you.

I clenched my core, seeking relief. None came. Only one thing would satisfy my hunger now.

Soft lips captured my earlobe, warm breath tickling my skin. His thumb brushed my nipple, and I groaned. I couldn't help it. I ground my bum against his erection. He hissed.

"Do that again," he muttered.

"Sebastian…"

His hand left my breast, traced down my side, and gripped my hip. He tugged me closer to him and rolled his hips, and this time, we both groaned.

I twisted in his arms, and he kissed me. No asking for permission, just raw, unapologetic taking of what he wanted, and I was lost.

Shivers racked my body, the trembles impossible to contain or stop. Feverish need arrowed between my legs the moment his tongue touched mine. His big hand covered my breast for the second time, his thumb circling my nipple through my satin camisole. Friction from the material combined with pressure from his thumb forced a moan to sound low in my throat.

"Tell me to stop." He kissed my neck. "Tell me you don't want this, that you don't want me. Tell me this is wrong."

I arched my back, pushing my hands into his hair. He tugged down on my top, his eyes fixed on my bare breast.

"I'm only a man. A man who's hanging on to the barest thread of control. Last chance to make this stop, Trinity."

His voice rasped, as if his vocal cords had been passed through a cheese grater.

"I don't want a last chance. I don't want you to stop."

He made this sound, almost as if he were in pain, then he sucked my nipple into his mouth. My head sank into the soft pile of pillows, and I closed my eyes. Wave after wave of scorching flames licked my body. I felt his lips on my other breast, then my stomach. He hooked his thumbs into the band of my knickers and slid them off.

"Jesus, you're so fucking beautiful."

I watched him staring right between my legs, and a flush of heat rushed through me. I strived for a suitable response to his compliment, one that didn't make me sound flippant. There were far more beautiful women than me in the world, but the way his eyes blazed as he said it told me he wasn't playing me. He meant every word.

As he dipped his head, I slammed my lids closed again. There was something almost too erotic, too... sensual, about watching Sebastian go down on me. Until a few weeks ago, we'd hardly spoken, and now he had his tongue on my...

Oh God.

My lips parted. I took panting little sips of air, and my heartbeat went into overdrive, hammering against my ribcage. My body took control, closing off my mind and shoving all awkwardness away. I raised my hips off the bed.

"Sebastian." His name spilled out of me on a breath of air. "More. God, yes, right there. Don't stop."

He did it again, that thing with his tongue. A kind of swirl and sweep that caused my clit to pulsate, an orgasm coming at me far too fast.

"I can't... oh... oh shit."

My body went rigid, and I tumbled over the edge. For a few seconds, I swear I blacked out, or at least entered a trance-like state that levitated my body and transported me somewhere else. I floated back to earth, and the first thing I heard was the rain, still unrelenting as it battered the glass. I became aware of my breathing, rapid but slowing. And then I opened my eyes.

"Hi," Sebastian said, his soft-gray eyes roving over my face.

He was lying beside me, yet I hadn't even been aware he'd moved. Too lost in the ecstasy of an orgasm so good, it should have been illegal.

"Hi."

I reached for him. He scooted away.

My chest pulled tight, and a horrible feeling settled in the pit of my stomach. "What's wrong?"

His tongue—the one that not very long ago had been between my legs—poked into the side of his cheek. And then he cleared his throat.

"I don't have any... I didn't think this would happen. I'm not prepared."

Ah.

"Bollocks," I said.

Sebastian choked out a laugh. "I love that word. Even more so when it comes out of your pretty mouth."

I gazed at him coyly. "We could... risk it." Yeah, all kinds of wrong, but I wanted him too badly.

"I have an idea."

He threw back the covers and got out of bed. My gaze dropped to his groin, the outline of his erection clearly visible through his cotton boxer shorts. A shiver of anticipation trickled down my spine.

"Where are you going?"

Opening the top drawer in the dresser, he grabbed a T-shirt and tugged it over his head. "Special forces are always prepared."

His intention dawned on me, and I stared at him, open-mouthed. "You can't."

A broad smile broke across his face. "Watch me."

22

S℩ʙᴀsᴛɪᴀɴ

You desperate fucker.

Yeah, I was, and I didn't give a shit. For two years I'd dreamed of getting Trinity into my bed, of knowing what it felt like to hold her in my arms, kiss her, taste her. Well, now I knew —and it wasn't enough. I longed to know every inch of her. I didn't want to wait for another time, one that might not happen.

Sully and Crew were already up and about when I got downstairs. They both looked at me with a questioning expression as I entered the kitchen wearing nothing more than a T-shirt and boxers. I held my hands in front of my groin—a necessary requirement.

"Morning, Mr. Devereaux. Something wrong?"

I opened my mouth to voice my request, but it stuck in my throat, Trinity's mortified expression coming back to haunt me. I wasn't in the least embarrassed, but the last thing I wanted was to make her feel uncomfortable. And who knew how long we'd have to stay here with these two ex-Special Forces servicemen? It could be days or weeks.

"Ah, yeah, I need to go out."

Here's hoping a half hour delay doesn't kill the buzz.

Crew arched a brow. "Wearing that?"

"Yeah. I mean no. I just wanted to let you know."

"No problem." Sully put down his coffee. "Where are we going?"

Ah, hell. I'd forgotten what they'd said last night about accompanied outings only.

"The grocery store, or a pharmacy."

Crew frowned. "If that's all, then one of us can go. There's no need for you to take a risk."

I released a heavy sigh. This wasn't going to work out. "Never mind." As I turned to leave, Sully called me back.

"Mr. Devereaux?"

I craned a look over my shoulder. "Yeah?"

His lips quirked on one side. "What size?"

It took me a few seconds, but as I figured out the meaning behind his question, I laughed. "Fuck. She's gonna kill me."

Crew caught up, chuckled, then zipped up his mouth. "Not a word to embarrass Miss Lane."

"Wait there," Sully said, skirting past me.

He returned in less than twenty seconds, handing over a ribbon of condoms. "These any good?"

Special Forces. Always ready...

I scanned one of the foil squares, noting the size. "Yeah, perfect."

Taking off upstairs, I pushed open the bedroom door, hoping like fuck Trinity hadn't changed her mind. I hadn't, that's for sure.

"You are a dead man," she said, but her eyes shone, and her cheeks were flushed, and when she threw back the covers and tapped the mattress, an open invitation to take up where we left off, I grinned, tore a condom packet off the strip, dropped the rest on the nightstand, and dove in beside her.

"Needs must."

I cut off her giggles with my mouth, sliding my palm along her jaw to angle her the exact way I wanted. Her pulse picked up its pace, and I grazed my thumb over it, feeling the juddering beat beneath her skin. She drew me on top of her, her hands cupping my ass, her legs wrapping around my waist. My dick glided between the folds of her pussy, my boxers the only barrier between me and her.

She wriggled her toes into the waistband of my underwear and shoved it over my ass. I yanked them the rest of the way down and tossed them on the floor. Skin to skin, I groaned. What I wouldn't give to slide home, no barriers, just me and Trinity.

I tore open the packet, pinched the end, and slid it over my dick. Trinity watched the entire thing through half-closed eyes, and I liked it. I liked her watching me. Fuck, I loved it. I'd dreamed of this moment for so long.

Don't screw it up.

I pushed inside her, and I found home. The fit. God, it was *perfect,* as if she'd been made especially for me, and I'd been made for her. Balls deep, I paused. Her eyelids flickered, then opened fully, and worry swam in her golden irises.

"What's the matter?"

"You're the girl, Trinity." I pecked her lips. "You're her."

Her forehead wrinkled, and then her eyes widened as she caught on to my meaning. "The one who got away?"

"Yeah."

Her eyes softened. "Oh, Sebastian."

I buried my face in her neck, covering her with kisses. I'd had two almost-serious relationships in my thirty-four years on the planet, one lasted four months and the other one three, but neither of those liaisons had given me this lightness in my chest and a sense of joy that completed me. Nor did they make me think about the future in a way I never had before. And since I'd first laid eyes on the woman beneath me, there'd been no one who'd interested me enough to even go on a date.

"Please move, before I go crazy," she begged.

"Maybe I won't," I teased, warmed by her giggles.

She clenched her muscles. I groaned.

"Okay, fine. You win."

I pulled out, and then, inch by torturous inch, I eased back into her, savoring every moment, committing this first time—the only first time we'd ever have—to memory. One I'd replay many times over, and remember how lucky I was to share this with her, the only woman I imagined spending my life with.

"You're enjoying this, tormenting me."

I repeated the movement, resisting Trinity's firm hands on my ass, urging me to speed up.

"If I go any faster, this will be over far too soon, and, like most men, I have a very fragile ego."

Her soft chuckle entrapped me, holding me hostage to her breathtaking perfection and her flawless beauty. I rarely conversed during sex. I wasn't particularly averse to it, but until now, intercourse had been all about the act, the climax, the sometimes awkward aftermath where I'd silently calculate how long I should wait before leaving. It wasn't like that with Trinity.

"Well," she mused, coyly biting her lip. "We're stuck here for the foreseeable. We have plenty of time to practice." She shot a glance at the ribbon of condoms I'd carelessly tossed on the nightstand. "And plenty of supplies." Her inner muscles fired up, holding my dick in a vise. "Now move, Sebastian."

I captured first one wrist and then the other. I held them over her head, gazing down at her for a beat. And then I withdrew and drove into her. I wasn't quiet. Neither was she. Nor was the bed. The mattress creaked and groaned, and the headboard rattled. The kitchen sat directly below this room which meant Crew and Sully were probably getting a free audible-only show. Not that I gave a shit. But Trinity might.

"We should be quiet," I said, burying my face in her neck.

"I think they know what we're doing, even without the bed chiming in." She groaned and then gasped when I angled my hips to brush her clit. "Screw 'em. Go faster. Maybe we can break the damn thing."

A laugh burst out of me, and the kind of happiness I'd never thought possible filled my chest.

"Challenge accepted."

I thrust my hips, catching her clit with each push forward. She sucked in little sips of air, her heels digging into my ass, driving me on. My balls tightened. I didn't know how I managed it, but I somehow held on until her muscles rippled and her climax erupted. I followed almost immediately, my release so powerful, the entire room spun, and white dots danced in front of my eyes. I freed her wrists and gathered her to me, holding her tight, riding out the seconds while my dick throbbed and jerked.

Rolling to the side, I discarded the condom then rested a hand on my abdomen and closed my eyes, waiting for my out-of-control heart rate to slow. When I caught my breath, I turned over, staring into Trinity's glowing golden irises. The tension around her eyes that she'd carried with her for weeks had disappeared. I cradled her face, the idea of lying here and not touching her striking me as ridiculous.

"You're the one," I repeated. "Ever since you walked into my life, I've known there'll never be another for me. I know we've got a tough road ahead, and we're drowning in shit right now, and I have no right to ask this of you, but I'm going to anyway. Be mine."

She sighed deeply. "Sebastian—"

I placed a finger over her lips, cutting her off. "Don't answer me yet. Take some time to think about it. I love you, Trinity. I've loved you for years. I don't expect you to say it back. We're coming at this from completely different places, and despite what you told me about your relationship with Declan, I know, at one time, he meant a lot to you. But I wanted you to know that however long I have to wait, I will."

She followed up another heavy sigh with a faint smile. "Can I be honest?"

A hollow ache in my chest chased away the earlier joy, and as much as I'd love to say, "No, lie to me. Tell me what I want to hear," I gestured for her to go ahead.

She pressed her hands together and tucked them underneath the pillow. Our faces were inches apart, yet I had the awful feeling that she was about to drive a huge stake through the delicate strands of our beginning.

"I told you about my upbringing, and how during my entire time living in children's homes, I dreamed of one day having a family of my own. At first, I prayed for a nice couple to adopt me, but when it became clear that was unlikely to happen, I couldn't wait to grow up and create a family of my own. And I'm not just talking about kids. I mean the whole extended family thing. I used to sit in my room at the home and imagine Christmases full of people and presents and too much food. When I met Declan, he swept me off my feet. He said all the right things, and he made me laugh. Then he introduced me to Serena and Justin, and I truly believed I'd found what I'd searched for my whole life. And you… you were so kind to me. I never could understand why Declan seemed to dislike you so much." She winced. "Sorry, that came out wrong."

My lips twisted, partly in regret that we hadn't reconciled our differences before he'd died. "No, you're right. We didn't get along. That's not a secret. To me, or to Mom and Justin."

Her eyes cast down, and she gave the smallest shake of her head. "I think he was jealous of you."

I laughed, trying—and failing—to keep the bitterness out of it. "I *know* he was jealous of me. The saddest thing of all is that I was ready and willing to help him. All I asked of him was to put in some effort, but the problem with Declan was that he wanted to take the easy route to success, especially as he assumed that's what had happened to me."

I didn't share how much it hurt that Mom always took his side, how, thirty-two years after she left me and Dad behind to live with her shiny new husband, it still cut me to the core. I hadn't even told Mom that's how I felt, preferring to brush it under the carpet. I worried that if I ever shared my deepest thoughts with her, I'd say things that couldn't be unsaid. In some ways, I blamed her and Justin for Declan's weakness. They'd pandered to him far too much. He lacked discipline, direction, and they'd always given him a safe place to land, and in my opinion, that had left him spineless and vulnerable.

"Here's the thing," Trinity said, jolting me from my musing. "These last few days spent with you have been wonderful. Truly. But the way you make me feel... it scares me. After what happened with Declan, I don't trust myself. I don't trust my feelings. What if they're false, triggered by everything that's happened? I'm scared that the shock of it all means my mind and my heart are deceiving me. I don't want to hurt you. I'd hate to hurt you."

"Hey," I crooned. "It's okay. I shouldn't have said anything. It's not my intention to heap even more pressure on you."

"You haven't. To hear you say you love me... it's wonderful." Her eyes misted over. "And I could love you so easily, Sebastian. Who wouldn't? You're gorgeous, kind, caring, have a body that shouldn't be legal, and you kiss me as if it's the last kiss you'll ever have. I just... I need more time."

I smoothed a hand over her hair. "Take all the time you need."

I'd wait. As long as it took, if it meant I had a chance to

make a life with her. Not for the first time, I cursed that Declan met her before I did. If it'd been the other way around, he wouldn't have stood a chance. I'd have made sure of it.

"You're doing that thing again. With your tongue, in your cheek."

I blinked, banished such pointless thoughts to the back of my mind, then grinned. "Is that so? Want to see what else I can do with it?"

She giggled, and I pounced, caging her with my body. I traced the outline of her rosy lips with the tip of my tongue. "How's this?" I bent lower and circled her erect nipple. "Or this." I edged lower, tracing the outline of her navel. "Or this."

She sighed contentedly and pressed her hand on top of my head, pushing me lower.

"You know what to do."

I smiled.

Yes. I did.

23

TRINITY

"What're you doing?"

I came around behind Sebastian, wrapped my arms across his broad chest, and rested my chin on his shoulder. On his computer screen were reams and reams of figures, each one blending into the next.

He twisted around for a kiss, and my heart did a little leap of joy. In less than twenty-four hours, our relationship had transformed from friends to lovers, and while I remained filled with self-recrimination and littered with doubts about how others would judge us, I also wanted to grab this slice of happiness while I could. At any moment circumstances outside my control might rip it away before I had a chance to build memories to last a lifetime.

"I'm neglecting you, aren't I?" He swiveled his chair and sat me on his lap. "I should be done here in a half hour or so, and then I'm all yours."

"I'm fine. You have to work." I peered closer at the computer. "What is all that?"

"It's the data behind a new study we've been carrying out into the effectiveness of one of our projects in Asia." He pinched the bridge of his nose, then massaged his eyelids. "We don't have anyone managing the Far East yet, so we share the work among the six of us. And this project falls under my remit. I'm going number blind looking at it."

"And here's me thinking the life of a billionaire was oh-so glamorous."

"I told you hearing about my life could cure insomnia. I wasn't joking." He grinned. "Oh, I have something for you."

He opened a drawer and fished inside, withdrawing a few sheets of paper bound with a paperclip.

"Here."

He handed them to me.

"What's this?"

"Confirmation that your debts are cleared. Declan's, too."

I pressed a hand to my chest. "Oh, Sebastian. I don't know what to say."

"There's nothing to say. I won't have you suffering for Declan's poor choices. Like I told you, he was my brother, my responsibility. It's done."

I dropped the bundle of papers on his desk and threw my arms around his neck, the constant niggling worry of impending financial hardship evaporating in a single act of kindness from a man who'd already given me so much.

"Thank you," I whispered in his ear.

He kissed my hair. "No, thank you."

"I-I don't suppose you've found out anything about my parents' things yet?"

He dropped his eyes, then shifted his gaze to the window. "Not yet, no."

Ah. It's bad news. They've hit a dead end, and he doesn't know how to tell me.

"No problem." I somehow managed to keep the disappointment from leaking into my voice. I'd raised my hopes, but I shouldn't have. Twenty years was a long time, and with very little to go on, it had been a long shot. "It's early days."

Sebastian's phone chimed with a text. He swiped the screen, scanning the message. "It's Loris," he explained. "They found the tracker. A tiny device slipped into the pocket of your coat." He blew out a breath, his cheeks puffing with air. "At least we know how they found us up in Scotland."

"One of them must have dropped it in there when they accosted me in that alley." I shuddered, thinking back to that night and how scared I'd been. How scared I still was, although less so with this particular bit of news.

"Hey." Sebastian smoothed a hand over my hair, then knocked up my chin with his thumb. "You're safe. Nothing's going to happen. They don't know we're here, and we have Crew and Sully. And either Loris or the private investigator will have news on the guns soon. I'm sure of it."

"Yeah, I know."

He reached forward and turned off the computer screen, then laced his fingers together and cracked his knuckles. "I'm going to pick this back up tomorrow. Let's go cook dinner, then after we've eaten, we can watch a little TV if you like." He chuckled. "See, I know how to show a girl a good time."

I grazed my fingernails over his jaw, day-old stubble scratching my skin. "There's not a lot else we can do."

"Oh, I don't know..." He twisted his head and kissed my palm. "I might have one or two ideas up my sleeve."

A pleasurable tremor echoed down my spine. "You've got quite the stamina."

He poked his tongue into the side of his cheek and raked

his gaze over me, finally settling on my breasts. He buried his head between them, sighing contentedly.

"I could stay here all night."

I palmed the back of his head, threading my fingers through the soft strands of his hair. "Eating might be difficult."

"There are other ways to satisfy hunger." He tugged down the top of my T-shirt and kissed the swell of my breast. "More enjoyable ways."

Groaning, I rolled my head and stretched out my neck. I sighed contentedly, and then my stomach grumbled. Sebastian's chuckle vibrated against my skin.

"I guess we'd better pick this up later and go eat after all."

He stood, righting me at the same time. The kitchen was empty with no sign of Crew and Sully. It mustn't be easy for those guys trying to stay out of our way. I'd bumped into them a couple of times today as I'd wandered from room to room, trying to amuse myself while Sebastian worked, but each time, they'd nodded briskly, checked I didn't need anything, then taken a diversion. I guess they must be used to this kind of thing, and it made me feel safe knowing there were three men in the house, just in case.

Sebastian moved around the kitchen as comfortably as if it were his own, and in seconds, onions, chicken, tomatoes, garlic, herbs, and a bag of fresh tagliatelle covered the countertop. I pulled out a chair and sat. Resting my elbows on the table, I propped my chin up with my hands and tracked his every move. His muscles flexed beneath the black T-shirt he'd chosen this morning, occasionally riding up when he reached up high, offering me a glimpse of smooth, tanned skin. I licked my lips at the sight of his toned abs, the inadvertent display making my mouth water.

He scooped up the chopped onions and dropped them into a frying pan where they sizzled on impact. Using a wooden spoon, he stirred them, then expertly flipped them the way I'd seen chefs do on TV. Damn, there was something hellishly sexy about a man who could cook.

"Sebastian?"

"Yeah?"

"Will you kiss me as if it was our last time?"

He froze, set down the knife he'd been cutting the tomatoes with, and wiped his hands on a towel. He strode toward me, cupped my face in his hands, and planted the kind of kiss on me that dreams were made of. My stomach tied itself in knots, my nerves humming like power lines, and my toes curled inside my shoes. I shoved my hands down the back of his jeans and gripped his arse. He groaned, the sound a rumble through his chest.

"What are you doing to me?" he murmured against my lips.

"Tormenting you," I replied with a smile.

"Carry on tormenting me, and you'll go hungry."

I dropped my gaze to his groin area, his excitement blindingly obvious. "Oh, I don't know. I'm sure I can find something to... satisfy me."

He groaned again. "Trinity. Jesus Christ."

I went for his button, flipped it open, and had my hand on his zipper when his phone rang. He shot a glance at it, then picked it up, wriggling away from me.

"Mom, hi."

My cheeks heated up. I'd almost forgotten who we were, who I was, the history I had with this family. We'd got caught up in a bubble where the outside world failed to exist, and Serena calling had burst that bubble in spectacular fashion. When she found out, she'd hate me. Justin would hate me. And what about Sebastian? Was he ready to deal with the fallout that we'd cause when all this came out? I wasn't at all sure that he was.

Another torrent of guilt raced through me. Declan died less

than a month ago, and I'd already fallen into bed with his brother.

What am I doing?

I scrambled to my feet, needing space and time to sort through my chaotic thoughts. I took two steps when I pulled up sharply at the alarm in Sebastian's voice.

"Wait, Mom, what do you mean someone confronted you in the street?"

I spun around, locking gazes with him.

"Trinity? No, I haven't seen her."

My eyes widened. Sebastian shook his head and held up his forefinger.

"Is Justin there with you?"

He paused while I tugged on the hem of my shirt. One-sided conversations were the worst. I could only guess what was happening.

"I'm sure it was nothing, Mom, but do me a favor and don't go out alone for the next couple of days. Yeah, okay. I'll call you in the morning."

He tossed his phone on the table, scuffed a hand over the top of his head, then laced his fingers together behind his neck.

"What? Tell me."

"Mom was on her way home from work, and a couple of guys stopped her in the street. Said they were looking for you. When she said she hadn't seen you, they threatened her. Told her to find you, and fast. Said they'd be back, that they know where she lives."

My knees buckled, and I steadied myself with a hand on the back of the nearest chair.

"Was it them?" I whispered, horror at the thought clenching my chest. I tried for a deep breath. Failed. Tried again, successfully this time.

"I'd say so." He tugged on his roots. "Fuck!"

"This is all my fault. All my fault. I've brought this on you, your mum."

"No!"

Sebastian reached me in two long strides, his hands clamping down on my shoulders. He shook me gently.

"For the umpteenth time, this is *not* your fault, Trinity. Declan brought these men into your life, into *our* lives. You're as innocent as I am. As Mom and Justin are."

"Why didn't you tell her I was here? Are you ashamed of me? Of us?"

"Jesus, no." He rubbed the back of his neck. "Far from it."

"I wouldn't blame you if you were," I said dully. "We both know how this—you and me—will look to people."

His face tightened, the skin stretching over his cheekbones giving him an even more angular, noble air. "I don't give two shits what anyone thinks." He tucked a strand of hair behind my ear. "I'm going to call Loris and have him put some protection around Mom and Justin until these guys are located."

He made the call while my brain ran through a multitude of scenarios, each one worse than the last. Now, Sebastian's entire family was caught up in this web of deceit, and although I agreed with Sebastian's assessment that it was Declan who'd brought this to our door, it didn't stop the guilt from tearing up my insides. I should have known what was happening, should have found a way to stop Declan from falling in with a criminal gang. We might have avoided all this if only I'd paid more attention and demanded answers to questions that I should have voiced.

"He's sending someone to watch Mom's house and follow her if she leaves."

I blinked several times, dragging my thoughts back to the present. I offered a wavering smile that didn't hold. "That's good."

"Hey." Sebastian's arms came around me, and he held me

tightly to his chest. "I am not ashamed of you, or of us, Trinity. One issue at a time, okay? Let's deal with the guns first, and then we'll figure out the rest. Together."

I sank against him, absorbing his strength, holding it deep inside my body for when I'd need to draw on it.

"Agreed?" Sebastian pressed when I hadn't answered after an entire minute scraped by.

"Yes," I said, my voice barely more than a whisper.

"Good." He kissed the top of my head. "Still hungry?"

I wasn't, but I nodded anyway. "Yeah."

"Right answer."

24

Sebastian

All night, Trinity tossed and turned, mumbling in her sleep. That Mom had become embroiled in this fuckup of Declan's weighed heavily on my shoulders, although I was confident that Loris wouldn't let any harm come to her or to Justin. But all of this weighed far heavier on Trinity's shoulders, and I hadn't yet come up with a way to take some of the pressure off of her. No matter how many times I reassured her that she wasn't to blame for any of this, there remained a significant belief deep within her that she did carry some culpability. In her mind, she'd kept to herself Declan's spiral into criminality, or at least her suspicion of it, and by doing so, she'd contributed to both his death, and the subsequent fallout.

I understood why she might think in those stark terms, but I didn't agree with her, and nor would I ever fully reconcile Declan's decision to take his own life rather than face up to what he'd done. All he had to do was reach out, and while I had to take some ownership for making him feel he couldn't come to me with his troubles, in the end, he, like all of us, was ultimately responsible for his actions.

As dawn broke, she finally settled. Her breathing deepened, and her chest steadily rose and fell. Tentatively, I climbed out of bed, picked up my cell from the nightstand, grabbed a T-shirt and sweatpants off the chair nestled in the corner of the bedroom, and tiptoed down the hallway to use the communal bathroom rather than risk waking her by using the en suite. Silence greeted me except for the pigeon that insisted on squawking loudly to announce its presence. I opened the window in the bathroom and shooed it away. Wings flapping, it rose gracefully into the air.

I showered, dressed and, leaving my hair wet and my jaw unshaved, I trudged downstairs. Coffee. That's what I needed. The whole world seemed better with a bloodstream full of caffeine. It did for me, anyway. I put on a pot, then dropped Loris a check-in text. He answered immediately, reassuring all was fine over at Mom's house, and that he was on his way to the safe house and to expect him in thirty minutes.

I sent back another. **Why? News?**

Crew and Sully appeared at the same time as Loris's response. **Yes.**

"Morning." Crew yawned loudly. "Boss is on his way over."

"Yeah, I know. He texted. He says he has news. What do you know?"

"Me?" Crew pointed at himself, then laughed. "We're the muscle. He's the chief. He tells us only what we need to know."

He picked up the pot of coffee before it'd finished brewing, and droplets dribbled, hissing and sizzling on the hot plate. Pouring three cups, he grabbed the milk from the fridge and set it on the counter, drinking his black.

"Heard about one of these fuckers confronting your mum," Sully said, adding a dash of milk to his coffee. "That blows, man."

"Yeah." I frowned. "How is it that you know?"

He grinned unashamedly. "We have a secure app that the Intrepid guys use. Zander, one of the guys that Loris sent to watch over your mum, dropped in an update last night."

"Us military types are the worst gossipers," Crew offered. "Don't sweat it."

I half smiled. "It doesn't bother me in the slightest."

Dodging around them both, I flicked on the electric kettle and made Trinity a cup of tea. I'd rather have let her sleep for a while longer, considering the restless night she'd had, but if Loris had news about the guns and the gang behind all this, then she deserved to hear it firsthand.

I opened the bedroom door. She was fast asleep, her legs tangled in the covers, her hair a wild tumble of browns and golds, contrasting with the stark white pillow. Setting down the tea on the nightstand, I gently shook her shoulder. She exhaled, her eyelids flickering.

"Hey, sorry to wake you. I brought you a cup of tea."

She groaned, rubbed her eyes, then sat up. "I had a terrible night's sleep."

"I know."

She peered at me. "You, too?"

"Yeah."

Picking up the tea, she blew on the hot liquid, then sipped. "Have you heard anything from Serena? Is she okay?"

"She's fine. I'll call her later." I played with a lock of her hair. "Loris is on his way. He'll be here shortly."

"He's found them?" She spoke in a whisper, and her fingers tightened around the cup.

"I'm not sure. He said he had news, so I'm guessing there's been a development that he wants to update us with."

I eased the cup of tea from her viselike grip, before she broke it, and set it on the nightstand. She clutched the sheets as a substitute, her knuckles turning white in the process.

"Why don't you get dressed and I'll make you some breakfast."

She shook her head. "Couldn't eat a thing. I'm too nervous. What if it's bad news? What if they can't find the guns? What will we do then?"

I put my arms around her and murmured soothing words. Eventually, her stiff body relaxed, and she let go of the bedcovers.

"I'm scared, Sebastian. I'm supposed to return to work on Monday. What will I tell my bosses if it's not safe by then? I can't afford to lose my job."

"Shh."

I rubbed circles on her back, swallowing words my instincts told me she wouldn't welcome. Every fiber of my body yearned to tell her that I'd take care of her. I'd take care of everything. That she never needed to worry about money ever again. I was certain an offer such as that would only alienate her. Since she was ten years old, she'd been alone, fighting to earn her place in the world. To blithely swoop in with a blank check would push her away when I had to keep her close. For her, yes, but mainly for me. I couldn't bear to contemplate a life without her at the center of it, and by shoving my wealth down her throat, I risked her freezing me out. She'd see it as an assault on her independence at a time when she might very well think that was all she had left in a life rapidly spiraling out of control.

I kissed her forehead. "One problem at a time, remember."

She gave me a wavering smile, her shoulders lifting with a deep intake of breath. "One problem at a time."

"That's my girl." I kissed her again. "I'll meet you downstairs."

I left her alone to shower and dress. She came downstairs at the exact time Loris arrived, her face pale, eyes wary. I pulled out a chair at the kitchen table and motioned for her to sit. She declined, tucking herself into my side instead. Crew and Sully lounged lazily against the kitchen countertop, their ankles crossed while Loris loitered in the doorway.

"Well?" I coaxed.

"We've located the guns," Loris announced as casually as if he was telling me the football results. "And the gang, including the leader. I've been in touch and arranged a rendezvous point to hand over the weapons."

Trinity froze beside me. I squeezed her hip in reassurance.

"When?"

"Tonight."

"Where?"

"That doesn't matter. Crew and Sully will stay here with you while the exchange takes place. I'll call you afterwards."

"I'm coming."

"No," Trinity exclaimed, her grip on me tightening. "I don't want you to go."

"Don't worry," Loris clipped. "He's not coming."

"Oh, I think you'll find I am."

Crew sniggered. Loris shot him a warning glare.

"Why do you want to come?"

"Because I want to look this fucker in the eyes and satisfy myself that once he has those guns back in his possession, that's it. All this shit is over. No more threats or intimidation. They go their way. We go ours."

"And you think I'm incapable of ensuring the same outcome?"

His eyes glinted in irritation. Too bad.

"You don't have skin in the game. I do."

Loris's icy gaze went to Trinity, then back to me. "Fair enough. If I were in your shoes, I'd probably feel the same way. But you do exactly as I tell you, got it?"

"Yeah. I got it."

"Sebastian." Trinity gazed up at me. "I don't like this."

"There's something else," Loris said. "It appears your

brother was also involved with drugs. About a year ago he started dealing, and over the last few months he took small incremental steps in an attempt to win a larger patch. When his current supplier struggled to keep up with Declan's ambitions, he sought a new supplier. Somewhere along the way, Declan ended up in debt. Maybe he was too ambitious and couldn't land enough clients to move the gear. It seems he stole the guns and planned to sell them to pay off his drug debts. But moving guns isn't as easy as moving drugs. My guess is he realized he was in over his head and that's why he chose to end things the way he did."

I sat there, stunned. Jesus. *You fucking idiot, Declan.*

Trinity gripped my forearm, and her entire body went rigid.

"But... but what if the drug gang comes after me?" she stuttered. "If the gun people can find me, then surely those other men can, too." She dug the heels of her hands into her eyes. "This will never end, will it?"

"It already has."

Trinity's eyes widened as she looked at me and then at Loris. "What do you mean?"

"I took care of it." He eyed me coolly. "I'll add the cost to your bill."

"Thanks. I think." I half smiled. "So when do we leave?"

"Ten o'clock."

"Sebastian, I really don't like this," Trinity reiterated.

I brushed my lips over hers. "Trust me. I'll be fine. By tonight, it's over. Done."

I hoped like hell that was true.

∼

Snow flurries swirled in the air, illuminated by the car headlights as we traveled toward the East End of London to the location where Loris had arranged for us to meet the gang members and hand over the weapons. Once Trinity was out of earshot, he'd given me the skinny on what he knew. The gang in question, originally from Liverpool, had recently moved into the area which meant, lucky for us, they weren't one of the larger criminal gangs that owned this part of London. From what Loris had gleaned, they were a small outfit, flying under the radar while they built their business, and this played in our favor. Loris believed that once they had their guns back, that would be the end of it. We'd discussed alerting the cops—it did not sit well with me to know I'd helped facilitate the distribution of illegal weapons—but Loris convinced me that would be the wrong approach. In his view, turning the gang and the guns over to the police was a sure-fire way to put my entire family, Trinity included, directly in the firing line. And I refused to do that. Family came first. Always.

Loris pulled off the main road onto a narrow lane and then turned onto a dirt track filled with potholes. My back jarred and my teeth rattled with each one we hit, but there were so many, they were unavoidable, even with Loris's expert driving. After around ten minutes had passed, a large building came into view. A warehouse, or maybe a barn of some kind, although there were no other buildings in the vicinity, so I doubted we were on a farm.

Loris eased the car to a stop directly in front of another vehicle facing us, its headlights shining right into our car. He cut the engine and waited.

The driver's door on the other car opened, and a short, wiry guy climbed out. He was younger than I expected. Mid-twenties, maybe, with an acne-scarred face and a ring through his right eyebrow. Two other men followed. They were around the same age as the first guy. I mused about their backgrounds, and what had gone so wrong that they chose a life of crime. Then again, Declan had come from a great home, and look how he turned out.

All three were carrying handguns, and the driver stood slightly in front of the other two.

Loris shot a glance at me, gave a curt nod, then reached into his holster and drew his weapon. He shoved open his door and climbed out, followed by the two others he'd brought along for backup. Loris held his handgun casually by his side. He must be a fast shot, if his relaxed stance was any indication. I sure hoped he knew what the fuck he was doing. Oh, who was I kidding? Of course he knew what he was doing. The man had *professional* written all over him.

The doors closed with a thud, muffling the staccato conversation outside. Loris also stood slightly ahead of his two bodyguards, and as I compared the three on our side to the three on theirs, I knew which side I'd rather be on. The apparent gang leader, or at least the leader of this cohort, pointed his chin in my direction, his lips moving in, what I guessed, was a question about who I might be, and why I hadn't gotten out of the car.

On the way over here, Loris had reiterated—several times—his orders for me to "stay fucking put until I say otherwise or I'll shoot you myself." I believed him, too. For all the aristocratic blood running through his veins and his fancy inherited title, Loris Winslow was a scary-ass bastard who didn't make idle threats.

Every second that scraped by felt like a minute, but eventually, Loris beckoned for me to join them. I slowly climbed out of the car, unashamed to admit how fast my heart was beating. I'd never been shot, and I'd rather keep it that way. Six men. Six guns. And me. A businessman far more familiar with a keyboard than a firearm.

"See this man here," Loris barked as I came to stand beside him, his voice filled with authority that slowed my pulse. "He's Declan's brother, the man whose death is on your hands. He's the son of the woman you threatened. He's the reason we're here at all. If it was up to me, I'd end every miserable motherfucking one of you, and you wouldn't even see it coming."

My lips parted. *What the hell is he doing?* The guy closest to me already looked as jumpy as fuck, his eyes darting left to right, his trigger finger twitching, and his two buddies shuffled from foot to foot as if the ground beneath their feet was on fire.

"You're here to make a deal, so let's make one," Loris continued. "You want the guns. I have the guns." His gaze dropped to the pistol in the leader's hand. It'd risen slightly, the barrel pointing up at forty degrees. "I also guarantee I'm a faster, better shot, and if you don't calm the fuck down, you're going to find out just how good I am."

The gun immediately lowered to his side, and I blew out the breath I hadn't even realized I'd been holding. Jesus, this could turn to shit in a split second, and we'd all end up dead or injured.

"My buddy here," Loris gestured to me again, "demands a guarantee that after we've completed the exchange, there are no follow-ups. It's over. Finished." The guy opened his mouth to speak, and Loris held up a finger. "Before you say a word, I'm going to make this easy for you. No guarantee, no guns. And trust me, friend, you do *not* want to make an enemy of me. If I so much as hear a whisper that you've come within a mile of his family or friends, or his fucking window cleaner, I will wipe out everyone you know while you watch." He jabbed a finger at the guy closest to us. "Including your heavily pregnant wife. And then I'll kill you. Slowly. Painfully. I'll take days to skin you alive."

I froze on the spot. The guy paled, and despite the freezing temperatures, his forehead beaded with sweat. Loris stepped forward and patted him on the shoulder, as if he was greeting an old friend.

"Do we have a deal?"

His head bobbed up and down at a rapid pace, and he dampened his lips, then swallowed.

"Deal."

My mouth went dry, and my leg muscles felt weak, the relief palpable. One look at this gang compared to Loris, and it was easy to see how out of their depth they were. Having seen their capitulation for myself in the face of Loris's stark and terrifying warning, I knew they'd never bother me or my family again.

Loris nodded at one of his guys who went around to the trunk and lifted out three black carryalls. He returned to us and dropped them on the ground.

"You may inspect them," Loris said.

The guy dropped into a crouch and unzipped each of the bags in turn. He straightened and faced the man on his right, dipping his chin in an acknowledgement that everything was in order.

Loris holstered his gun, then gripped the lead guy's shoulders, his fingers digging into the tendons and muscles. "Remember what I said. I'd hate to cut up your pretty wife's face." A malevolent smile curved his lips at the edges. "But don't doubt that I will. One word that you're not holding up your end of the bargain, and..." He drew his finger across his neck. "You feel me?"

He swallowed and blinked, then dampened his lips. "Yes."

"Good."

The four of us got back into the car, and Loris reversed, then headed back down the bumpy lane.

"Do you believe him?" I asked, seeking that last scrap of reassurance. "Is it really over?"

Loris nodded crisply. "He thinks he's running with the big boys, but he's not even a mid-lister. Sometimes, though, they can be more dangerous. The true criminal gangs who run the East End have honor, rules that they, and the men they hire are expected to live by. But not these guys. They probably sank all their cash into those guns, and that's why they were so determined to recover them. Now that they have, you won't see them again."

I released a deep breath. "I'd appreciate it if you wouldn't mind keeping watch on my mom for a few more days."

"You got it." He side-eyed me. "You want me to ask Crew and Sully to stick around for a day or so with you and Miss Lane?"

"No. I'll take Trinity home with me, but I'll call you if anything feels off."

He held out his hand, and I shook it. "Nice doing business with you. My bill is in the post."

I laughed, an unexpected release of tension relaxing the tight muscles across my shoulders and back. "Happy to pay every penny."

25

Trinity

My feet hurt, and my knees ached from all the pacing. I had no nails left, so I'd started biting my skin, and now my fingers were sore and bleeding. I fired a desperate look in Crew's direction. His hands shot in the air.

"Don't ask me. Not again. I already told you I'm as much in the dark as you are. They'll get here when they get here, and you wearing out that rug won't make the time go any faster. Now sit your backside down." He kicked out a chair. When I remained standing, he shook his head and shrugged. "Suit yourself."

"Do these things usually take as long as this?"

"These things? Honey, it's not paint by numbers."

"But what if they're in trouble?"

He laughed, a proper belly laugh that showed off a set of brilliant-white teeth. "Clearly you don't know Loris."

"No," I snapped. "Clearly I don't." Swiping a hand over my face, I sighed. "Sorry, I'm overwrought."

"No apologies necessary."

He gestured to the chair again, and this time I sat.

"Loris Winslow is one of the toughest sons of bitches I know, and I know a lot of tough sons of bitches. Unless this gang leader has a death wish, he'll take the guns, scurry down the hole he crawled out from, and be thankful that he escaped with his balls still attached to his body."

I smiled at the image he painted. "How do you know him?"

"Loris?"

I nodded.

"I served under him in Syria and Afghanistan. When he tapped out after his sister died and started Intrepid, he told me if I ever wanted a job, there'd be one waiting." He lifted his shoulder in a nonchalant gesture. "How could I refuse?"

"Do you miss it? The military?"

His lips quirked at the edges. "Sometimes, yeah. I guess I miss the camaraderie most of all, although Intrepid has filled a hole in that regard."

"How many people work at Intrepid?"

"You ask a lot of questions."

I grinned. "It helps to keep my mind off what might be happening. I can go back to pacing if you'd prefer."

He pressed his palms together in fake prayer. "Please God, no. Not that. Anything but that."

I plucked a grape from the bowl on the table and threw it at him. He caught it easily, popping it into his mouth.

"Assault with grapes. I should call the cops."

I smiled wider. I liked Crew. A lot. And Sully. I'd miss them when all this was over—if it ever *was* over.

"To answer your question, I haven't a clue how many of us there are working at Intrepid. Although Loris only started the company three years ago, it's grown at a fast rate. He has bodyguards working all over the world."

"All former military?"

"Yeah. He hires the best of the best." He laced his fingers, extended his arms, and cracked his knuckles. "Hence, he hired me."

"That's quite an ego you have there," I teased.

"Honey, you have no idea."

Sully appeared at the entrance and knocked on the doorframe. "They're back."

I scrambled to my feet so fast, the chair tipped over. I righted it, then raced to the front door. Crew and Sully's enormously wide shoulders blocked my view. I rose on tiptoes but still couldn't see. My mouth was dry, and I felt unsteady on my legs, my knees trembling and almost knocking together.

The two men parted. Right in front of me stood Sebastian. With a cry, I threw myself at him and, uncaring of the audience, I kissed him hard on the mouth.

"Jesus," Sully muttered. "My old lady never greeted me like that when I arrived home after a nine-month tour, let alone after a couple of hours' absence."

"Hence you divorced her," Crew said.

"True."

"Let's go inside," Loris urged, motioning with his arms.

He closed the door behind him, and we filed into the kitchen. I refused to release Sebastian, my hand wrapped tightly around his arm. He took a seat and pulled me onto his lap. In other circumstances, I might have felt the heat of embarrassment creep up my neck, but I was so glad to have him back in one piece, I didn't care what anyone thought.

"What happened?" I looked at Sebastian, then up at Loris, then back at Sebastian. "Did it go okay?"

Sebastian ran his hand over my hair. "Everything went fine. Loris gave them the guns. It's over."

I wanted to believe that, more than anything, but a niggle inside my head wouldn't let up. If they had the guns, then we'd lost our leverage. What was to stop them coming after us, to silence us? I voiced as much to the men crowded into the small kitchen.

"They won't," Loris insisted. "I know they seemed scary to you, but to me, they're little more than kids out of their depth."

"He put the fear of God into them," Sebastian grinned. "They'd be idiotic to try anything, although I've asked Loris to keep his men watching over Mom for a few more days, just to be on the safe side."

"And what about me?" I whispered. I hadn't said anything to Sebastian, but the idea of going back to the flat filled me with dread. It would always be the place where Declan had killed himself, and I knew I'd never sleep in that bedroom again.

"You're coming home with me," Sebastian said.

My shoulders sagged, and my head tipped forward as I blew out a slow, relieved breath. "I won't overstay my welcome, I promise. I'll start looking for a flat immediately, but I just... I can't bear to go ba—"

"Guys, can you leave us, please," Sebastian barked, cutting me off. "I think I need to have a stern word with my girlfriend."

Girlfriend?

Crew and Sully sloped off while Loris promised to call in a couple of days. As soon as we were alone, Sebastian locked his gaze on mine.

"Does what's happened between us these past few days mean so little to you?"

My lips parted, and I touched them with my fingertips. "No, of course not. What are you talking about?"

"You honestly thought I'd let you go back to that apartment?" He cradled my jaw, running the pad of his thumb over my cheek. "I won't push you into anything. If you don't feel ready to move in with me, then that's fine. I'll help you look for a place, one in a safer neighborhood than your current one, but there is no way you will *ever* return to the home you shared with Declan."

"M-move in?"

His face softened. "Trinity, I've already told you I'm in love with you, that I've loved you for more than two years. Of course I want you to move in, but only when you want it as much as I do. I'll wait for you, as long as it takes, but I'm serious about us. You're it for me, and I hope in the not too distant future, you'll feel the same. I know things are moving fast, but life is short. If Declan has taught either of us anything, it is precisely that. But until I'm satisfied that those guys have truly left us alone, I'm not letting you out of my sight."

Stunned, I said the first thing that came into my head. "I have to return to work on Monday."

"I think you should call your boss and tell him you need another week off. I don't mean to lay down the law, but with the job you do where you're out and about visiting people, it makes sense to give it a little longer."

I couldn't argue with his logic, and I had enough annual leave to cover the additional time off. "Okay, I'll call him first thing Monday morning."

He curved his hand around the back of my head and pulled me down for a kiss. "Let's go home."

"Now?"

"Now."

～

Sebastian dropped our bags inside the front door and securely locked it behind us. I appreciated the gesture, despite his and Loris's hefty reassurances that the gang wouldn't come around here. Not today, not ever. I accepted it would take me a little while before I truly believed the nightmare of the past few weeks was over.

I rubbed my neck muscles. Everything ached. My back,

legs, shoulders. And I had the beginnings of a tension headache.

"Why don't you take a bath while I call Mom and check in," Sebastian said, taking over massaging my neck.

I dropped my head and gave myself over to how damn good that felt. "Will you tell her about... us?" The tentative tone of my voice gave away the inner turmoil hidden behind such an innocent question.

"Not yet."

I twisted around, and his hands came to rest on my hips.

"Why not?"

Even though I was relieved he didn't plan on blurting it out before I'd prepared myself, I was interested in his reasoning. I fully expected it to come as a shock to them. Hell, it still shocked me that I'd ended up here, with Sebastian, and I knew how distant me and Declan had grown these past months. Serena and Justin thought we'd been happy, and the thing I feared most was that they'd blame Sebastian and he'd end up ostracized because of me.

"Now isn't the time. You've been through a hell of an ordeal, and Mom will be feeling edgy after what happened to her. Let's just wait for things to settle down and then we'll go and see them together." He pecked me on the lips. "Stop worrying."

"What makes you think I'm worried?"

He traced his thumb between my eyebrows, smoothing the skin. "This, right here." Swatting my backside, he grinned. "Now go run a bath. Use the one in my bedroom. It's at the far end of the corridor, to the left at the top of the stairs."

"Why that one?"

He waggled his eyebrows. "It's big enough for two."

Despite the bone-deep weariness dogging my every step, I mustered a bright smile. "Good. I need someone to wash my back."

He chuckled, swiping at my arse again. I skipped out of

reach and hauled myself up the stairs and along the hallway to Sebastian's bedroom. The room was decorated in navy blue with accents of cream and bronze, and as I toed off my shoes, my feet sank into the luxurious carpet. I breathed in deeply. The room smelled of Sebastian. Clean and fresh, with a spicy undertone. I trailed my fingers over the soft cotton bedding, imagining slipping between the sheets and having Sebastian wrap his arms around me and kiss and touch and fuck me. I pondered whether it'd feel different now that we no longer had the threat of danger hanging over our heads. Maybe the constant worry had heightened our attraction and with the arrival of 'normal', and with nothing to sustain them, our feelings would wither and die.

I shook my head, laughing at my fanciful musings that had no basis in reality. As each day passed, I became more and more sure that my feelings for Sebastian were real. He'd unreservedly admitted he was in love with me, and while I'd kept my cards close to my chest, I was mature enough to recognize that I was falling for him, too. There was something about Sebastian that called to me, an overpowering sense that I'd found... home. I'd never felt like that during my entire relationship with Declan, not even in the beginning when lust had consumed us.

I opened one of two doors on the far side of the bedroom and entered an enormous walk-in wardrobe lined with suits and shirts, trousers and belts, and enough pairs of shoes to give most women a run for their money in colors of brown and black, and most shades in between.

"And I thought I liked shoes," I muttered. Not that I could afford many pairs, but those I had, I cherished.

I retraced my steps back into the bedroom and opened the second door. This time, I successfully located the bathroom.

Jesus.

It was *enormous*, with twin sinks—for a man who lived

alone?—a gigantic walk-in shower, and a tub that'd easily fit four or five, let alone the two Sebastian had alluded to. It also had power jets, the kind that spas had. I turned on the mixer tap and glanced around. No bubble bath, but I spotted one of those bath bombs. I lifted it to my nose. It smelled of strawberries. I wondered if Serena had bought it for Sebastian as a Christmas present. It didn't strike me as the kind of thing he'd purchase for himself.

I dropped the bath bomb into the water. It fizzed as it dissolved, turning the water a very pale pink. I chuckled, imagining Sebastian's reaction when he saw that. Yeah, he *definitely* hadn't bought that for himself.

Slipping out of my clothes, I folded them and set them on top of the closed toilet seat. I bent over the tub and tested the water. *Ouch*. Too hot. I adjusted the temperature, running my hand underneath the water. Better.

"Now, that's a view."

I whirled around, automatically wrapping my arms across my chest. Pointless really, considering Sebastian had explored pretty much every inch of me. He unfurled my arms, pushing both of them behind my back where he held my wrists in his hand. And then his gaze flickered over my shoulder.

"What the hell is wrong with the water?"

I giggled. "I found a bath bomb on your shelf over there. It adds color, but smells nice, too. And they're great for your skin. I guessed right that you didn't buy it, then?"

"No. Probably Mother. I don't honestly recall where it came from."

"What did she say? Is she all right?"

He skimmed the tip of his nose down mine, his lips close enough to take. "She's well. Coolness personified, actually. Very little rattles my mother. I said I'd drop by tomorrow."

"Did she mention me?"

"She asked if I'd seen you."

"And what did you say?"

"I told her that I had, and you were fine."

I breathed noisily through my nose. "What do you think she'll say, when we tell her?"

"I have no idea." He feathered my lips with a barely there kiss. "She'll be surprised, I expect. You really do need to stop worrying. We can't live our lives in fear of what other people may or may not think. If she or Justin have a problem with you and me, then it's up to them to deal with it."

I wished I had it in me to be so nonchalant. I'd always been a worrier, and I doubted I'd ever stop. But my primary concern here wasn't for me; it was for Sebastian. Even though his parents split up when he was very young, he still had a mum and a dad who both adored him. He'd never known what it was like to be truly alone, and I hated the idea that I might cause issues in his family. I wasn't sure what I'd do if Serena and Justin reacted angrily to the news that Sebastian and I were together. I hoped it wouldn't come to that.

I wriggled myself free of Sebastian's hold, then ran my hand through the water. Perfect. I stepped into the tub and sank beneath the water, groaning in pleasure. Sebastian stripped and casually dropped his clothes on the floor. "Move forward," he instructed, and when I shuffled up a bit, he climbed in behind me. His muscular thighs caged mine, and he hooked his ankles over mine, pulling my legs apart. He covered my breasts with his hands and gently kneaded them while his lips took a leisurely journey across the back of my neck. My skin tingled, and I let my head fall to the side, resting against his shoulder.

"Feels good?"

I sighed in pure bliss, my earlier disquiet scattering under his tender touch. "So good."

He released my right boob, then trailed the tips of his fingers between my cleavage, over my stomach where he drew leisurely circles around my navel. He moved my ankles even farther apart, opening me fully to him. He caressed between my legs, his touch featherlight. I closed my eyes and allowed the remaining tension to float away. Concern for the future could wait until tomorrow. Right now was all that mattered.

"I never dreamed I'd get to be with you, to touch you in this way. To make you mine. And you will be, Trinity. Mine. I'll wait as long as it takes for your feelings to catch up to where I am. I don't doubt for a second that you will. Eventually."

He cupped my jaw and maneuvered me to face him. His expression, so open and honest, and filled with awe, was the final straw. The shaky walls I'd built crumbled, leaving me bare to him.

"I'm already yours."

26

SEBASTIAN

"You'd better have a damn good reason for calling me at this ungodly hour on a Saturday morning?"

"Oh, please," I said to my fellow ROGUES board member, Garen, who sounded as alert as ever. "Everyone knows you never sleep, and you *always* work on weekends."

"That was before I had something to stay in bed for."

I smirked. "Say hi to Catriona for me."

"I will. Now what do you want? And make it snappy."

I grinned to myself, unperturbed by Garen's bark-is-worse-than-his-bite attitude. "I need a favor."

"Go on."

"Can you take a look at the Japanese project? I'm going number blind and I'd appreciate a second pair of eyes."

Out of all the ROGUES, Garen was the smartest when it came to math. The fact he had a photographic memory and an ability to see patterns in rows upon rows of numbers was what I needed to make sure I'd called this one right.

"What's your gut telling you?"

"A projected twenty percent return in the first year alone."

Garen let out a low whistle. "If you're even half right, that's a hell of an ROI."

"Isn't it? And given what's been going on with me and my family right now, I want to make doubly sure I haven't fucked up somewhere."

"Send it over. I'll get right on it."

"Thanks. I appreciate it."

"How are things? At home, I mean."

I hesitated to tell him the full story. Not yet. He was completely unaware of the torch I'd carried for Trinity for so long, and I'd rather keep it like that for the time being while it was all very new. And as for the troubles that had surfaced since Declan's death, only Upton was aware. I'd kept the rest of the ROGUES board in the dark, carrying on as normal. Working, attending meetings, delivering as I always had. I'd give them the full picture when I was ready and not a moment before.

"They're okay. It's difficult, as I'm sure you can appreciate."

"And your mom? How's she holding up?"

"Resilient as ever."

"Gotta be tough, though, man. To lose her son. And for you to lose a brother. I know you and Declan weren't all that close, but still…"

"Yeah."

When I said nothing further, he got the message, clearing his throat.

"I'll call you Monday at the latest with an update. You still intending to present the findings at the board meeting on Friday?"

"That's the plan." A light tap on my office door brought my head around. I motioned to Trinity to come in. "Gotta go, buddy. Thanks for stepping up. I appreciate it."

"Hang tough."

"Always."

I ended the call, tossed my phone on my desk, and held out my arms to Trinity. She sat on my lap and wrapped her arms around my neck.

"I don't mean to disturb you."

I swept a hand down her jean-clad thigh and squeezed her knee. "You can disturb me anytime."

She beamed, and my insides lit up like Times Square on New Year's.

"I've booked a restaurant for tonight. Seven-thirty. I thought it might be nice to get out of here."

She frowned. "Are you sure it's safe for us to go out?"

I'd worried this might happen, that Trinity would want to hide away, and after all she'd endured, I couldn't blame her. But that wasn't the answer. It was important for her to get out there and realize she was completely safe.

"I'm positive. You weren't there last night, but you have to trust me, and trust Loris, that those guys are out of your life. They're never going to bother you again."

She drew her bottom lip inside her mouth. "But you still have Loris's guys watching your mum. That must mean you're worried."

"And I'm watching you." I ran my eyes from her head to her toes, lingering on her chest. "And what a sight it is."

She palmed my shoulder and laughed. "You're nuts."

"Nuts about you." I pulled her down for a kiss.

"Is this a fancy-pants place?" she asked. "I don't have any nice dresses or things like that."

I chuckled at her description of a fine dining restaurant. "It's a bistro. Jeans and a top are fine. Tomorrow, I'll drive you over to your place and we can pack up the rest of your things. Then you can give notice to your landlord." I held up my hands before she worried I was trying to coerce her into moving in after I'd promised not to press her. "I don't want you living there, no matter what you decide. If you want more time on your own, that's absolutely fine. I'll help you find a nice place that's close by here."

She snorted. "I doubt my measly salary will afford a garage around here, let alone a flat."

"We'll cross that bridge when we come to it," I said, loath, at this juncture, to offer to subsidize her rent.

"Okay. And thank you. I hated living there after..." She held my gaze, her face flooded with sorrow. "Sometimes, when I try to go to sleep at night, I still see him..." A swallow forced its way down her throat. "I don't think I'll ever erase the memories."

"You will. One day."

"I wish I'd told you. I wish more than anything that I'd told you of my concerns the night I turned up here. If I had, then maybe he'd still be alive."

Tears pooled in her eyes, and I hated it. I hated that she cried for him. And I hated myself for thinking that.

"Please stop torturing yourself. It's killing me. You did what you thought was right at the time, and we'll never know what the outcome might have been if you had told me."

"Declan would still be alive," she whispered.

"You don't know that. Declan made his choices. He could have come to me when he realized how much trouble he'd gotten himself into, and yet he didn't. And who knows? If you had told me, he might have taken out his wrath on you. He was in a desperate situation, and sometimes, that causes men to do desperate things. But his death is *not* on your hands, and it's not on mine. The fault for Declan's death lies with him and with the men who made him feel as if he'd run out of options."

A few seconds passed by where she reflected on what I'd said. I couldn't fix Trinity's guilt for her. Hell, I had enough of my own to deal with, but somehow, I'd convince her that she wasn't to blame, no matter how long it took me. And maybe the inquest would go some way to making her feel better.

"I hear you," she eventually said.

"But do you believe me?"

Her eyes locked on mine. "Yes, I believe you."

∽

Trinity sauntered across the kitchen, her high-heeled ankle boots clacking on the floor, her long legs poured into a pair of black skinny jeans. She'd paired the smoking-hot bottom half with a V-neck plum-colored sweater that outlined her perfect breasts and narrow waist. Her hair lay in soft waves over her shoulders, and she'd added a touch of makeup to her eyes, cheeks, and lips.

"Fuck me," I rasped.

"Well, I can, but that'll make us late."

I broke into a mile-wide smile. Trinity spent so much time worrying about things outside of her control that when she shook off the manacles and relaxed, I couldn't love her more. I hoped, as time went by, she'd show more of this side and worry far less about what other people may or may not think.

"I can wait." I grabbed my wallet and keys. "Ready?"

"Yes."

I opened the passenger door for her, noticing how she surreptitiously glanced around her before getting in. I guessed it would take a while before she stopped looking over her shoulder and expecting those guys to confront her, but in time, she'd shake off the fear and move forward—and I'd be right there by her side.

I parked on the street a few minutes from the restaurant. I gave my name to the greeter, and she showed us to our table, a booth by the window, as I'd requested. Our server came over shortly afterward, and we ordered our food and drinks—water for me, a gin and tonic for Trinity. After the server retreated, a momentary silence fell, and then Trinity smiled.

"This feels weird."

"Why?"

She shook her head. "I don't know. I guess it's been full-on for so long, and we haven't really had much time to... be."

"Yeah, I guess you're right." I reached for her hand and folded it in mine. "We have all the time in the world. We can take it slow, or go fast, or somewhere in between. Whatever you're comfortable with."

"Can I tell you something?"

"Always."

"I wish I'd met you first, too."

A band pulled tight around my chest, and my stomach clenched. "We're here now."

The strained atmosphere melted away, and as every minute crept by, my happiness grew. We chatted about all kinds of things from our favorite movies, to food likes and dislikes, to places we'd love to visit one day. I locked away every scrap of information and hung on to each word as if it might be the last time I ever heard her voice.

Replete and with Trinity a little tipsy, we left the restaurant just after ten and moseyed down the street toward the car. Feeling like a horny teenager on my first date, I stopped outside a coffee shop and maneuvered her against the door.

"What are you doing?" She giggled.

"Copping a feel."

I unzipped her coat and burrowed my hands underneath her sweater. Her nipples immediately puckered, and I crowded her to protect her from the brisk wind.

"What if someone sees?"

"Who cares?" I swooped in for a kiss, my tongue demanding entry.

She opened up to me without hesitation. Blood hummed

through my veins, and my dick jerked inside my jeans. I must have kissed her for a full minute, and when we broke apart, both of us were breathless.

"I need to take you home before we get arrested for lewd conduct." I fixed her sweater back in place and zipped up her coat. "There. It's as if I haven't ravished you at all."

She grinned. "Race you to the car."

She set off, her heels clacking on the sidewalk, her giggles floating on the breeze. I caught her easily and wrapped my arms around her waist, lifting her clean off the ground.

"Next time, try sneakers."

I kissed her again. I appeared incapable of keeping my hands off of her, almost as if I needed constant physical contact to make up for the two years I'd suffered in silence. "God, I love you," I murmured, our lips still connected.

"What the *hell* is going on?"

I twisted around and groaned. "Justin. What are you doing here? Shouldn't you be with Mom?"

I caught Trinity's horrified expression out of the corner of my eye. I drew her into my side. Justin's eyes flashed in fury.

"How long has this been going on?" He gestured between us as if we needed the additional physical sign to know what he meant.

"Not long." If he expected me to show the slightest embarrassment or shame, he'd have a long fucking wait.

"Before or after your brother killed himself?" he snapped, spittle gathering at the corners of his lips.

"If you have to ask that, then you don't know me or Trinity at all."

"No. Evidently, I don't." He landed his enraged gaze on Trinity. "Declan only passed away a month ago, and yet here you are, bold as brass, with your tongue down his brother's throat."

"Now hang on—"

"No." He jabbed a finger in my chest. "You hang on. I guess I shouldn't have expected much from you. Declan always was a thorn in your side, you petty bastard. But you." He pointed at Trinity. "I expected more from you."

"I'm so sor—"

"Don't you dare apologize," I cut across her. "You have nothing to apologize for. We're not doing anything wrong."

"Legally, no," Justin snapped. "But morally?"

I snorted a laugh. "You talk about morals? If you knew what we—"

"Sebastian, no!"

Trinity clutched my arm and shook her head violently. "Please, don't."

Justin's eyes narrowed. "Don't what?"

The only thing that stopped me from telling him just what kind of man his precious son had been was the plea in Trinity's eyes. All she cared about was protecting the feelings of others, while consistently neglecting her own.

"Forget it." I sliced my hand through the air.

"Your mother will be so disappointed in you."

I jammed my hands into my coat pockets for fear of breaking his face. I'd tolerated Justin, just like he'd tolerated me, but we'd never been close. Hitting him, though, would upset Mom, and so I kept them buried.

"She'll understand."

"Will she? You're a traitor," he spat. "And she," he pointed at Trinity again, "is a whore."

I moved, all earlier thoughts of hurting Mom vanishing in a mist of red. My hand wrapped around his throat, and I shoved him up against a parked car. The alarm blared, the side lights flashing, and a couple across the street stopped and looked over.

"If you ever speak to her like that again, I will kill you."

"Sebastian, stop, please," Trinity pleaded. "Stop this. Both of you."

I squeezed tighter, and only when his eyes bulged did I release him. I rose to my full height, giving me a good five-inch advantage. "That wasn't an idle threat. You know *nothing*. And if you want to stay in your idyllic little bubble, you'll show Trinity some respect, otherwise, regardless of her wishes, I will blow your sad little life wide open."

I gripped her elbow and propelled her toward the car. Settling her inside, I walked around the back of the car and peered down the street. Justin was still there, where I'd left him, glaring in my direction. I got into the car, started the engine, and drove away.

"Are you okay?" I cast a sideways glance at Trinity, then refixed my attention on the road. "Talk to me. Are you all right?"

"Oh God, Sebastian. This is awful." She shifted her position, her eyes settling on my face. "You can't tell them."

I clasped her stiff fingers in mine and squeezed. "We might not have a choice. I will not have him or anyone else talk to you like that."

"You can't blame him."

"Oh, I can."

She fell silent, and when I released her hand, she pulled it close to her chest. For the remaining journey home, she stared out the window and repeatedly gnawed on her bottom lip.

I parked the car outside the house, and together, we went inside. I helped her with her coat and hung it inside the closet in the hallway. "Do you want a drink?"

She shook her head. "I think I'm just going to go to bed."

The tiredness in her tone made it clear she'd rather be alone. As much as it pained me, I let her go, my eyes tracking her up the stairs. As she approached the top, I held my breath, wondering which direction she'd turn. If she went to the right, then my heart might snap in two, because my bedroom was on the left.

She turned left.

Suppressed air exploded from my lungs. *Thank God.*

I poured a glass of whiskey and tried to organize my scattered thoughts. By the time I got to Mom, Justin would have shared his poisonous views. I could only hope she'd hear me out, and I didn't have to shatter her memories of Declan.

I wouldn't bet a red cent on the outcome.

27

TRINITY

I went to bed alone, and woke alone, with no idea whether Sebastian had slept beside me. His side of the bed was cold, although that meant nothing. He might have simply arisen early. I hadn't expected to get a wink of sleep, but after going over and over what had happened with Justin, and how to fix it, exhaustion had won out, and I'd sunk into a dreamless sleep.

Swinging my legs over the side of the bed, I sat there for a few minutes to gather my thoughts. I already knew what I had to do, but knowing and doing were two completely different things. It wouldn't be easy. It *would* be painful. I used the bathroom, hastily dressed, then went downstairs. I found Sebastian sitting at the breakfast bar, a mug of coffee on the counter, his iPad propped up in front of him on what appeared to be a news channel. He looked up as I appeared, and his loving smile ripped a hole in my heart.

"Morning. Sleep well?"

"Like the dead."

He slipped off the stool and kissed me. And I let him. Another traitorous act on my part.

"I worried I'd wake you when I came to bed."

Ah. So he had slept beside me. God, this was awful. I needed to move things along before I broke down.

"I'd like to go over to my place now, please." *Before I lose my nerve.*

The space between his eyebrows puckered in a frown. "What's the rush? Don't you want breakfast first?" When I shook my head, he added, "Or a cup of tea at least?"

"No."

His gaze bored into mine, and no doubt, a dozen questions filled his mind. He didn't voice a single one of them.

"Okay. I'll get my coat and we can go."

I followed him outside and pulled up the collar on my coat to stave off the stiff February wind. Spring was still some way off, and the sky was gray, the clouds low and heavy, befitting of my mood. Sebastian locked up and walked to where he'd parked his car in front of his house, opening the passenger door for me. I got in, and so did he. Neither of us spoke. Me, because if I did, I'd cry, and Sebastian, I guessed, was waiting for me to smash the wall I'd erected. He hadn't a clue what was coming, and even though I was about to break his heart, I couldn't see an alternative solution.

As we turned onto my street, my stomach twisted and my tongue felt thick and awkward, as if it had swollen to twice its size. Sebastian stopped the car and cut the engine, then twisted in his seat to give me his full attention.

"What's the matter?" he asked. "You're too quiet, and you're worrying me. Is this about last night? Please, Trinity, say something."

A swell of tears pooled in my eyes at his gentleness and patience.

"I'm so sorry," I sobbed, unable to hold back the tide for a moment longer.

"What for?"

"I can't do this."

His entire face relaxed, the worry lines gathered around his eyes smoothing. "You don't have to do this. I'll do it. You can stay in the car. I'll leave the engine running so you don't get cold."

Perplexed, I frowned, and then I caught up with the misunderstanding, and a fresh wave of dread took root in my gut.

"You don't understand. I mean us. I can't... I can't be with you."

I covered my face so I wouldn't have to see the dismay on his. He gripped my wrists and tugged my hands down, giving me no choice other than to confront him.

"If this is about Justin—"

"It's about your family, Sebastian. I lost mine, and I know how painful that is. You have your family, and I won't be the cause of you losing any more of them."

His lips thinned, and a nerve beat in his cheek, the one he often poked his tongue into whenever lost in thought.

"Justin is *not* my family. To me, he'll always be the man who stole my mother from me and my father. I am civil to him for my mother's sake. No more, no less."

"But your mum *is* family."

"I'll talk to her. She'll understand."

"She might not. And what will you do then?"

"I choose you," he said. "I'll always choose you."

My chest ached, and I pressed a fist to it. "And that's why I have to be the one to end this."

"No!"

He gripped my shoulders and shook me.

"Don't do this. Please. Mom will understand. She will."

"Even if she does, Justin won't. Wherever we go, people will stare and whisper behind our backs and judge us. It doesn't matter that things were over between Declan and me long before he died. All people will see is that I jumped into bed with the brother—the rich brother—right after Declan passed away."

He shoved jerky hands through his hair. "That's just optics. I don't give a shit what anyone thinks. And I certainly don't give a flying fuck about Justin."

"But I do," I whispered. "I could live with acquaintances judging me, but I can't deal with causing issues in your family. Call me weak, but I can't live with that."

"You are not weak. You're one of the strongest people I know."

The way my insides were crumbling, I disagreed. I didn't feel strong. I felt frail and pathetic. But whatever Sebastian said about his mum and Justin, losing a family member, whether through the final cruel act of death like I had with my parents, or an ostracization, as Sebastian was at risk of, was the worst pain in the world, and I refused to be the reason Sebastian lost his mum as well as his brother.

"I'm sorry, but nothing you say or do will change my mind."

The fact that he'd said he'd always choose me meant I had to be the strong one, even if my actions hurt him. The hurt would recede, eventually. I opened the door, but not before I saw pain score his face. The image would haunt my dreams for a good long while.

"Please don't stay here. Not here. I'll find you somewhere. Somewhere better."

My instincts screamed at me to turn around, to take the selfish path and steal him for myself even if it cost him his family, but I couldn't do it. Not to him. Never to him.

"Goodbye, Sebastian."

I hurried inside and slammed the door, bracing myself against it. A few seconds later, the unmistakable throaty roar of

Sebastian's car reached me and, with a squeal of tires, he drove away.

I slid down the door to the floor and pulled my knees to my chest. I glanced around at the flat that hadn't been a home in so long with silent tears tracking down my cheeks. This was the last time I would allow myself to cry. Tomorrow, I'd begin the search for a new flat. I'd lose the security deposit on this place, which meant I'd have to eat into my overdraft again, but it'd be worth it. I couldn't stay here, that was certain.

A new, lonely future stretched out ahead of me. But as lonely as it might be, I took a morsel of comfort in knowing I'd done the right thing, and that alone would carry me through the tough days and weeks ahead.

28

Sebastian

Blue lights and the unmistakable sound of a police siren brought me to a stop five minutes away from Mom's house. I cursed and cut the engine. Taking a deep breath didn't help with the churning in my gut, and as the cop approached and tapped on the driver's-side window, staring down at me with that practiced sanctimonious expression they all seemed to wear, I had to bite down on my tongue. The urge to get to Mom's and have it out with her and Justin meant I'd lost track of how fast I was going, and now, I'd suffer further delays, which was the very last thing I needed. I would not lose Trinity. I could have stayed behind and continued the pointless argument through a closed door, but in truth, the only way to win her back was to talk to Mom and get her blessing. Mom wasn't like Justin. She'd understand. I knew it.

Stay calm. Answer his questions. Get the fuck out of here.
"Yes, Officer?"
"Is this your car, sir?"

"Yes."

"Do you know how fast you were going?"

No, but you do, so let's cut the crap and give me the goddamn ticket.

"I'm afraid I don't. My mind was elsewhere."

"A dangerous occupation, don't you think, sir, given you're behind the wheel of a powerful motor car."

He raked a disapproving gaze over the sleek lines of my Mercedes AMG coupe, and it took everything I had in me not to roll my eyes.

"Yes, Officer."

"Can I see your driver's license, please?"

I reached into my jacket and took out my wallet. Holding it open at the see-through pocket where I kept my license, I showed it to him. He took it from me, perused it, then looked from it to me and back to it again. I fidgeted in my seat, and my hands gripped the wheel until my knuckles went white.

The cop narrowed his eyes. "In a hurry are we, sir?"

Fuck's sake. That's why I was speeding, dickhead.

"Not particularly."

"Hmm." He gave the license another once-over, then handed my wallet over. "I'll let you off with a caution on this occasion, Mr. Devereaux, but please remember that the streets of London are not a racetrack."

Prick. "Yes, Officer."

I scratched my cheek and stared straight ahead until he walked away, and then I eased my car into the traffic and stuck religiously to the speed limit for the rest of the way. There wasn't a space outside Mom's house, so I parked a couple of streets over. I took one look at her face when she opened the door and muttered, "Justin told you, then."

She nodded and stood back, motioning me inside. I shrugged out of my jacket and hung it on the coat rail, then followed her into the kitchen. Justin and I locked gazes, but it might as well have been horns. He glared at me, and I returned the favor with interest.

"I want to talk to Mom. Alone," I added pointedly.

Justin glanced at Mom, and whatever he saw in her expression caused him to storm out. Mom sighed and sat at the kitchen table. I pulled out a chair and sat across from her.

"What did he tell you?"

"That he saw you and Trinity kissing in the middle of the street and when he challenged you, you didn't deny that you were in a relationship."

"What else did he say?"

"Not a lot." She held out her hand, and I took it. She squeezed me tightly. "I'd rather hear from you, anyway. Do you love her?"

"Yes."

She nodded. "I thought so."

I frowned. "Really?"

"I used to watch you watching her. Your eyes followed her everywhere she went. Admittedly, you weren't in her company very often, but when you were, it was like nothing else existed for you. She eclipsed everything in your orbit. Is she in love with you, too?"

I hope so. "I think she might be, yes. I know this looks bad, but Trinity and Declan were having problems long before he died."

"I'm aware."

I should have known. Mom had a sixth sense about most things, especially when it came to her kids.

"How come?"

"He told me. I called him out once, about six months before he died, for snapping at her over nothing, and after he'd barked at me to keep my nose out of his business, and I informed him that as my son, everything he did was my business, he admitted that he thought she didn't love him anymore, and he was losing her. I told him I agreed and if he wanted to keep her, he'd better start treating her better."

My mother sure was an indomitable force, one to be reckoned with. Not much got past her.

"Darling, I was aware of Declan's faults all too well. I loved him with all my heart, and I always will. He was my son, but he had a fatal flaw, one he couldn't get past no matter how much he tried."

"And what's that?"

"His jealousy of you."

This wasn't news to either of us. Declan had never hidden his envy of my achievements from any of us. "He drove me crazy, Mom, but I still loved him. We weren't close, and I have to take some of the blame for that, but I just wanted him to man up, to show some grit and determination. He wanted the easy way out, and I wanted him to work for it."

"It pains me to admit it, but Declan wasn't strong like you are, darling. He tried, but in the end he wasn't built that way. He adored you, but he'd never have admitted that to you. Strangely, he had this entrenched belief that I loved you more than him, and so he sought to punish you by behaving the complete opposite to what he saw as your expectations of him."

Mom's words were like a blow to the gut. So many times, I'd had exactly the same thought, and as much as I'd always kept my feelings to myself, Mom had opened the door and I walked through it.

"I always thought you loved him more than me."

"Oh, darling." She tilted her head to the side, her ear almost touching her shoulder. "When you have children of your own, you'll realize that you love them equally. It's impossible to love one of your children more than another."

"I felt abandoned when you left Dad."

Fuck. It's all coming out now.

Her face twisted in pain. "I know. And I've always blamed

myself for that. But, darling, trust me, it was the right decision. Your father and I would have made you terribly unhappy if we'd stayed together. Two happy parents living apart are far better for a child than two unhappy parents who stay together for the sake of that child."

Her logic was sound, even as I wished things had been different. Dad had never remarried. Mom was the love of his life, and he'd found no one to match up to her in his eyes.

"I'm sorry I never made more of an effort with Declan. I tried, but..."

"I know you did."

I stared out the window. "Trinity has broken things off."

Mom gasped at the suddenness of my confession. "Why?"

I snorted. "Why do you think? Because of what Justin said. She's gotten this thing in her head that you'll cut me out of your life because we're together."

"I'd never cut you out of my life. You're my son and I love you."

I knew it.

A swell of relief swept through me at her acceptance of the idea of me and Trinity together. With Mom on our side, surely Trinity's fears would have no basis for her to cling to.

"It's not me you have to convince, Mom. While I originally fought my feelings for Trinity out of my loyalty to Declan, in the end, I realized that life is for the living. If Justin can't get over his small-minded judgements and wish us well, that's his issue. The problem I have is that Trinity doesn't feel the same way. I'm sure you know that she grew up without a family, and she's terrified of being the cause of me losing mine. Losing you, basically." *Because I don't give a shit about Justin.* "And she worries about the optics, about how others will see and judge us."

"If you think it will help, I'll talk to her. Reassure her I only want the two of you to be happy."

"I don't want to cause any more problems between you and Justin."

"Pah." Mom flicked her wrist dismissively. "I've been dealing with that man for years. I know exactly how to handle him. He's hurting, like we all are, and he took that out on you and on Trinity. It was a shock for him, that's all."

"He called her a whore, Mom."

Her lips thinned. Evidently, that was news to her. She sat up straighter, her gaze flicking in the direction Justin had gone.

"Like I said, you leave Justin to me." Her voice had taken on a hard tone. "And besides, since when have I ever put up with anyone telling me what I can and can't do?"

I grinned. "Let me see. That will be never."

"Precisely."

A moment of silence fell between us, and it gave me time to make a decision. Mom deserved to know at least the bare bones of the truth about Declan's suicide, so it didn't come as a shock at the inquest. I didn't plan on telling her just how far he'd fallen. But it didn't feel right keeping it from her entirely.

"Mom, about Declan and why he... did what he did. I had someone look into it, to see if we could uncover his reasons, especially as the note he left told us nothing. It seems that Declan had gotten himself into debt. He owed a lot of money to some not very nice people, and I guess he couldn't see a way out." I lowered my chin to my chest and shook my head sadly. "That he felt he couldn't come to me is something I will never forgive myself for."

Mom took a moment to let that sink in, and then she reached over the table and gently tilted up my chin. "Please don't, darling. Declan didn't have to come to you. He could have come to me or his father, yet he chose not to." She touched the cross hanging on a thin chain around her neck, a Christmas gift from Declan a few years earlier. "Is that why one of those men stopped me in the street asking about Trinity?"

I nodded, even though that wasn't the entire truth. I'd never purposely tell her about Declan's involvement in drugs and firearms, regardless of what I said to Justin last night in a moment of anger. She deserved to keep her memories of Declan exactly as they were rather than tainted with the truth. "They wanted Trinity to pay for Declan's debts. I paid them off instead."

She stopped playing with the necklace and dropped her hands into her lap, staring at them for a long minute. And then she stood and brushed her hands over her hips.

"Right, I am going to make breakfast. And once we've eaten, you are going to head over to see Trinity and prove to that girl that you won't let anything or anyone stand in the way of your happiness."

I stood and hugged her, the air between us finally clear after so many years of hidden hurt. It hadn't been easy to tell her how I felt, but now that I had, a weight had lifted, and I knew that our relationship would only get stronger from here on out.

"Wise words from a wise woman, Mom."

She patted my cheek as if I were still ten years old. "I'm glad you've finally realized, darling."

29

Trinity

I stared at my pale and blotchy face in the bathroom mirror, then splashed it with cold water. After patting myself dry, I returned to the bedroom. My gaze automatically went to the ceiling fan, and I shivered as hazy images that I'd pushed to the outer edges of my mind came into focus with horrendous clarity.

Less than two hours had passed since Sebastian left—at my request—and already I missed his steady influence, his calm demeanor, his impish grin, and the way he stuck his tongue into the side of his mouth. I missed his kisses and his strong arms cradling me. I missed it all.

A voice inside my head, quiet at first, grew ever louder until it screamed at me to call him, to tell him that I'd made a terrible mistake and beg him to forgive me and take me back. Maybe he was right and Serena would be okay with the idea of me dating her eldest son, but Justin never would. I'd seen it in his face, clear as a crisp dawn on a winter's day, that he'd see us burn in

Hell rather than accept us as a couple. I couldn't face splitting a family in two for the benefit of my own happiness.

Sebastian thought he didn't need his family, that he had his friends, and his business, and he'd have me, and it would be enough. But I knew differently. Over time, maybe months, maybe years, he'd grow to resent me for cleaving his family in half with him on one side of the divide and them on the other. He'd deny it, of course. I'd expect him to. Most people never appreciated what they had until they no longer had it, and I refused to be the one to teach Sebastian that painful lesson, even if it came at a heavy price to myself.

When my parents died, I came to understand that a broken heart caused physical pain, not just emotional distress, yet I'd wrongly assumed that a heart could only break once. But the sharp pain slicing across my chest and compressing my lungs was stark evidence to the contrary. Except I had no rights to these feelings. I'd been the one to end things between me and Sebastian. Now I had to live with the consequences of my decision.

I jumped at a knock at the door. How long would it be before my nerves weren't constantly on edge? Despite the reassurances from Loris that those men wouldn't bother me anymore, without Sebastian's protective shield around me, I felt exposed.

Ensuring the chain was in place, I unlocked the door and opened it a crack, my heart rate slowing as I recognized the uniform of a local courier company.

"Miss Lane?"

"Yes?"

"I have a delivery for you."

Delivery? I'm not expecting anything. My gaze dropped to a medium-sized box tucked under his left arm.

"Hold on." I closed the door, removed the chain, then opened it again.

"Sign here, please."

He passed me the electronic device, and after I signed, he swapped it for the box. I thanked him and closed the door, then slotted the chain back into its housing.

A thick band of parcel tape ran down the center of the box and along the sides. I took the package into the kitchen and removed a sharp knife. Slicing through the tape, I set the knife down and folded back the four pieces of cardboard.

I peered inside.

A photo album? At least that's what it appeared to be. I tucked my fingers down the side and lifted it out, revealing a crisp, white envelope with my name scrawled on the front. I set the album on one side and slid my nail underneath the sealed flap. Removing a single sheet of paper, I unfolded it.

I planned to give this to you tonight, but things didn't work out as I hoped. I wish I could be there to see your face when you open it.

All my love.

Sebastian.

I turned my attention to the album. With trembling hands, I skimmed a palm over the soft brown leather, then opened it.

"Oh my God."

Nestled inside a thick piece of cream card was a picture of my parents, a photograph I'd never seen before. They looked young. Early twenties, maybe. I flipped the protective tissue that separated the pages. Another picture, this time of my mum holding a baby. Me. She stared into the camera with shining eyes and a serene expression.

My vision blurred with each page I flipped over. How had he done this? I reached the end, counting twenty pictures in total, including one of Mum and Dad on their wedding day. Closing the book, I picked it up and hugged it to my chest. Of all the gifts in all the world, nothing would ever beat this. Even if I lived to one hundred, I'd treasure this photo album as if it were a priceless artifact. To me, that's exactly what it was.

Sebastian. I have to see him.

Using extreme care, I returned the album to the box and sprinted across the living room. I wrenched open the door.

"What the...?"

I skidded to a halt. Flowers and balloons festooned the small path leading up to my flat. Assailed with the sweet smell of roses, lilies, and God only knew what else, I searched the street. My eyes fell on him standing a few feet away. My breath caught in my chest as he spread his arms out wide.

"I'm not leaving. Not without you."

A few passersby stopped and gaped at us, and my next-door neighbor—who I'd never spoken to—appeared on her front step and openly gawped as if we were some kind of freak show.

"The album... Sebastian, it's beautiful. I'll treasure it forever. How did you do it?"

"My guy called me yesterday and told me he'd located a few of your parents' possessions in a government storage unit, including two photo albums. Some of the pictures were unsalvageable, but I had him work through the night restoring what he could. As I said in the note, I planned to give it to you tonight after you'd moved your things into my place, but after the stunt you pulled this morning, I had to change up my plans and call a courier who agreed to a rush job. The rest of their things are being boxed up and shipped to my place tomorrow."

I pressed a fist to my sternum. "I-I don't know what to say."

"I spoke to Mom, Trinity. It's all good. The only thing standing in the way of our happiness is you."

A sob crawled into my throat, emerging as a strangled sound that propelled me forward. I tore down the path and into his waiting arms.

"I love you." I covered his face in kisses. "I love you so much. Is your mum really okay?"

Chuckling at my exuberant public display, he skimmed his nose down mine then planted a kiss on the tip. "Really truly okay. Not that it would have mattered to me. I'd never have let you go, no matter how hard you pushed me away. Somehow I'd have persuaded you that we were worth fighting for."

"Oh, yeah?" I arched an eyebrow. "And what if I'd still resisted?"

His lips turned up on one side. "Then I'd have kidnapped you."

∽

Four Months Later...

"Oh, look at the ocean. It's beautiful. And that beach." I swiveled in Sebastian's direction. "I love it."

"After the wedding, I'll take you sightseeing. I'm not a huge fan of LA per se, but once you get outside of the city, the surrounding areas, the beach communities and, in particular, the mountains, are spectacular."

"I can't wait." I nibbled on the skin around my thumbnail until Sebastian tugged my hand from my mouth. "Sorry," I murmured. "I'm nervous, that's all."

"There's no need to be. Everyone is excited to meet you. They're annoyed at me for not bringing you out sooner. What can I say? I'm a selfish ass who wanted to keep you all to myself."

I'd met Sebastian's father at Easter time when he came to London for a visit, but so far, I hadn't met any of Sebastian's ROGUES colleagues, or their significant others, and now that the time had come to take the plunge, a swirl of nerves circled in my stomach. Apart from his parents, these people were family to Sebastian, and it meant everything to me that we got along.

"Relax, Trinity. They're all boringly normal."

I nodded and forced a smile. The anticipation was the worst. As soon as I met them all, I'd feel much better.

I hope.

We traveled north along the coast road toward Malibu, where Belle and Upton's wedding was being held at their home. After forty-five minutes, the car stopped in front of a set of imposing gates, and the driver rolled down his window and announced our arrival. The gates opened, and he drove through. He stopped in front of a three-story house standing within impressively manicured grounds. Another bite of nerves took flight in my belly. I dove into my bag and found a tissue that I used to wipe my damp palms.

"We'd better get inside before you collapse from a heart attack," Sebastian joked, earning a fierce glare for his troubles. "Come on, gorgeous."

I emerged from the car into brilliant sunshine. Sebastian joined me and, with my hand firmly encased in his, we walked over to the house.

"Hey, Barbara," Sebastian said, enveloping her in a tight one-armed hug. "This is Trinity, my girlfriend. Trinity, this is Barbara, Upton's housekeeper and the only woman apart from Belle who can keep him in line."

I held out my hand, and she shook it. "Pleased to meet you."

"And you, sweetheart. I'm glad you're here, Sebastian. Upton is having something of a panic attack." She raised her eyes to the ceiling. "Men. Honestly. Belle is the epitome of serene control, yet he's paced so much this morning that he's going to need to invest in new carpeting throughout. Maybe you can calm him down."

"I'll do my best," Sebastian said.

We followed Barbara into the house, and while a "Wow" was on the tip of my tongue as she led us through Upton and Belle's vast, beautiful home, I managed to suppress it. Wealth on the scale that Sebastian and his friends enjoyed was still something I hadn't quite got used to, and I wasn't sure if I ever would.

"He's in here." Barbara opened the door to a vast room with wall-to-wall bookshelves, each one crammed with books.

A tall, dark-haired, and very handsome man whirled around as we entered. Sebastian had already warned me about the scar that Upton suffered after getting caught up in a terrorist bomb a few years ago, but all the mark did was enhance his beauty rather than detract from it.

"Jesus, thank God you're here. I'm freaking the fuck out."

He shook Sebastian's hand, then hugged me. "You're a brave woman, Trinity, taking on this jerk, but damn, am I happy to meet you."

"What's with the freak out?" Sebastian asked. "You're aware you're marrying Belle, right? The woman you've been living with for almost two years."

Upton made a face. "Yes, I'm aware." He rolled his eyes. "See, Trinity, I told you he was a jerk."

My earlier nerves dissipated, swept away by the warm welcome. If the rest of Sebastian's friends were as nice as Upton, I really did have nothing to worry about.

"Where's everyone else?" Sebastian asked.

"They're in the backyard. Belle's upstairs with her mom. I've been told, in no uncertain terms, that if I dare set one foot on the second floor, I'll be attending my funeral rather than my wedding." He grinned at me. "And that's the woman I'm marrying. Come on, let's introduce you to the rest of the motley crew."

As it turned out, everyone *was* as nice as Upton and, with the last vestiges of anxiety well and truly put back in their box, I took my seat beside Catriona, Garen's girlfriend, while Sebastian, Upton's best man, stood beside him at the head of the makeshift aisle. It wasn't long before the traditional 'Wedding March' sounded. The entire congregation twisted in their seats to watch Belle walk toward her future husband, her mum on one side of her, and her brother, Zak, on the other, balancing on two crutches. Sebastian had explained that the same bomb blast that injured Upton and killed his sister also resulted in Zak suffering a spinal cord injury. Initially paralyzed from the waist down, as time went by, he'd regained some feeling in his thighs and, with leg supports and crutches, he was able to walk beside his sister on her wedding day. The entire story had brought a tear to my eye. Life was full of trauma. As I grew older, I learned that it was how we dealt with it that was important, and Zak's strength in the face of such adversity humbled me.

When Belle joined Upton, Sebastian sought me out. Our eyes locked, and he mouthed, "We're next."

A wave of intense emotions rushed through me, and my heart swelled to twice its size. *Marriage? Me and Sebastian? Yes, please.*

The ceremony wasn't a long, drawn-out affair, and before too long, Upton and Belle headed back down the aisle, her arm tucked inside his, their expressions blissful. Sebastian strolled up to me and stuck out his arm for me to take, but instead of following the guests to the waiting marquee where they intended to hold the wedding breakfast, he led me in the opposite direction, away from everyone else.

"Where are we going?"

He ignored my question and led me around the side of the house. Once we were out of sight, he stopped. Urging me against the wall, he placed his hands on either side of my head and slowly moved in. When his lips hovered a couple of inches from mine, he paused.

"They looked so happy, don't you think?" he murmured, his gaze on my mouth.

"Yes." My breath caught in my throat, especially when his gaze traveled farther down to the rather impressive cleavage I sported. I blamed this dress, or maybe the pushup bra I'd invested in. Either way, right this second, I appeared to have made a solid investment.

"Belle made a beautiful bride," he continued, moving tantalizingly closer.

"She did." My lungs flattened, and I grew lightheaded as I waited for him to make his move.

"But not half as beautiful as the bride you'll make."

"God, Sebastian," I groaned. "Will you kiss me already?"

His lips twitched, his slate-gray eyes darkening with desire.

"I will, as soon as you've answered one question."

"What's that?" I panted.

"Will you marry me and let me spend the rest of my life taking care of you?"

Tears of joy sprang to my eyes. Six months ago, I hadn't known where to turn, and I'd stayed with a man I no longer loved for fear of losing the family I craved. And now I had all the family I'd ever need. Sebastian, Serena, the ROGUES guys and their wives and girlfriends. Even Justin had started to come around, making a groveling apology a couple of weeks ago, one I'd accepted without hesitation.

"Only if I can take care of you, too."

"Deal," he murmured.

And then he kissed me.

THE END

Thank you for reading ENTICED. I hope you loved Sebastian and Trinity's story. I have loved every minute I've spent with the ROGUES, and I hope you have, too.

Wait! Before you go, I have exciting news. Would you like to know more about Loris Winslow and his team of hot, sexy, alpha bodyguards that make up Intrepid Security Services? Well then, you're in luck. GUARD OF HONOR, the first book in the Intrepid Bodyguard Series is now available for preorder.

A woman on the edge of insanity—or is something far more sinister at play?

A year ago, Honor Reid was kidnapped and held hostage for seventeen days. Freed in a ransom drop gone wrong, her ordeal has lasting consequences. Despite round-the-clock security, she lives in fear of her abductor returning to finish the job.

Royal Marine veteran, Aiden "Mack" McKenzie isn't interested in a babysitting job on the other side of the Atlantic, especially for a billionaire heiress who point-blank refuses to leave her house.

When the man Mack owes his life to pleads with him to take the job, Mack reluctantly agrees. However, he gets more than he bargained for when he finds himself drawn to the woman he's bound to protect.

Within days of his arrival, strange things start to happen, and Mack must face up to the possibility that the woman he's falling for is not all she seems.

Available on Amazon

BOOKS BY TRACIE DELANEY

The Winning Ace Series

Winning Ace

Losing Game

Grand Slam

Winning Ace Boxset

Mismatch (A Winning Ace Spin Off Novel)

Break Point (A Winning Ace Novella)

The Brook Brothers Series

The Blame Game

Against All Odds

His To Protect

Web of Lies

Draven (A Brook Brothers Spin Off)

The Brook Brothers Complete Boxset

Irresistibly Mine Series

Tempting Christa

Avenging Christa

Full Velocity Series

Friction

Gridlock

Inside Track

Control (A Driven World/Full Velocity Novel)

Full Velocity Boxset (Books 1-3)

ROGUES Series

Entranced

Enraptured

Entrapped

Enchanted

Enthralled

Enticed

The Intrepid Bodyguard Series

Guard of Honor

Stand-alone

My Gift To You

ACKNOWLEDGMENTS

I am extremely fortunate to be surrounded by a team of people who love and support me and adore my stories to the extent that they do.

Hubs - thank you for allowing me to fly free and follow my dreams.

To my critique partner, Incy… Thank you so much for your commentary on this novel. We might not agree on everything, but you always give me pause for thought and that's invaluable.

To my wonderful, funny, kind, generous, amazing PA, Loulou for your unending support. I'd hate to walk this path without you.

Emmy - thank you for your terrific editing as always.

Katie - giiirrrllll! Thank you. Thank you. Thank you. I appreciate every second you are willing to spend reading and giving me your razor-sharp insight. Truly, you're one in a million.

Jean - Is it November yet! Gah, can't wait to see you and hug the life out of you!.

Jacqueline - Thank you for reading, as always. I appreciate you so very much. Looking forward to when we can meet up for a coffee - please let it be soon!

To my ARC readers. You guys are amazing! You're my final eyes and ears before my baby is released into the world and I appreciate each and every one of you for giving up your time to read.

And last but most certainly not least, to you, the readers. Thank you for being on this journey with me. It still humbles me to think that my words are being read all over the world.

If you have any time to spare, I'd be ever so grateful if you'd leave a short review on Amazon or Goodreads. Reviews not only help readers discover new books, but they also help authors reach new readers. You'd be doing a massive favor for this wonderful bookish community we're all a part of.

ABOUT TRACIE DELANEY

Tracie Delaney realized she was destined to write when, at aged five, she crafted little notes to her parents, each one finished with "The End."

Tracie loves to write steamy contemporary romance books that center around hot men, strong women, and then watch with glee as they battle through real life problems. Of course, there's always a perfect Happy Ever After ending (eventually).

When she isn't writing or sitting around with her head stuck in a book, she can often be found watching The Walking Dead, Game of Thrones or any tennis match involving Roger Federer. Coffee is a regular savior.

You can find Tracie on Facebook, Twitter and Instagram, or, for the latest news, exclusive excerpts and competitions, why not join her reader group.

Tracie currently resides in the North West of England with her amazingly supportive husband and her two crazy Westie puppies, Cooper and Murphy.

www.authortraciedelaney.com

Printed in Great Britain
by Amazon